"If you can, I suggest a warm bath,"

Thane said.

Bath! Meghan's mind screamed. Thane's expression was innocent of anything but concern—but they were alone, together. "I think a blanket will warm me."

"Don't you trust me, Meghan?"

"It's me I don't trust. I'm afraid I might forget the ground rules of this friendship. Next thing you know I'll be asking if a kiss is permissible."

"You wouldn't," Thane said.

"I might."

"Are you thinking about trying to seduce me?" he asked.

"*Could* you be seduced?"

His voice was low as he said, "Highly likely..."

Dear Reader:

The spirit of the Silhouette Romance Homecoming Celebration lives on as each month we bring you six books by continuing stars!

And we have a galaxy of stars planned for 1988. In the coming months, we're publishing romances by many of your favorite authors such as Annette Broadrick, Sondra Stanford and Brittany Young. And that's not all—during the summer, Diana Palmer presents her most engaging heroes and heroines in a trilogy that will be sure to capture your heart!

Your response to these authors and other authors of Silhouette Romances has served as a touchstone for us, and we're pleased to bring you more books with Silhouette's distinctive medley of charm, wit and— above all—romance.

I hope you enjoy this book and the many stories to come. Come home to romance—for always!

Sincerely,

Tara Hughes
Senior Editor
Silhouette Books

MARCINE SMITH

Murphy's Law

Silhouette *Romance*

Published by Silhouette Books New York

America's Publisher of Contemporary Romance

For special people:
my parents, Phil and Stella,
friend Caryl,
and, as always, Daryl

SILHOUETTE BOOKS
300 E. 42nd St., New York, N.Y. 10017

ISBN: 0-373-08589-3

First Silhouette Books printing July 1988

Printed in the U.S.A.

Books by Marcine Smith

Silhouette Desire
Never a Stranger #364

Silhouette Romance
Murphy's Law #589

MARCINE SMITH

lives on a farm in northwest Iowa with her husband and three of their four sons. She loves reading; writing romances; watching baseball, basketball and football; long drives through the Iowa/South Dakota countryside and the smell of freshly mown hay. But her favorite things are sharing the porch swing with her husband at dusk of a summer's day, watching the sun set and listening to the corn grow.

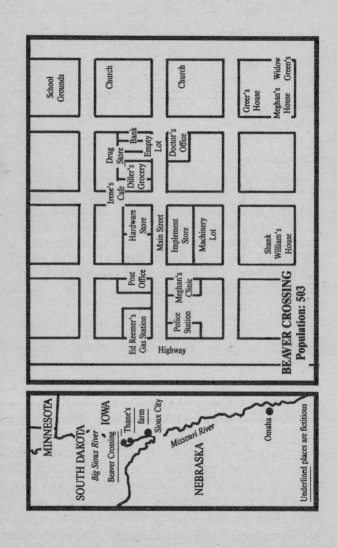

School Grounds

Church

Church

Greer's House

Meghan's House

Widow Green's

Irene's Cafe

Drug Store

Bank

Diller's Grocery

Empty Lot

Doctor's Office

Hardware Store

Main Street

Implement Store

Machinery Lot

Shank William's House

Ed Reemer's Gas Station

Post Office

Meghan's Clinic

Police Station

Highway

BEAVER CROSSING
Population: 503

MINNESOTA

SOUTH DAKOTA

Big Sioux River

Beaver Crossing

IOWA

Thane's farm

Sioux City

Missouri River

NEBRASKA

Omaha

Underlined places are fictitious

Prologue

Once Meghan Forester, D.V.M., parked her four-wheel-drive pickup in front of the Beaver Crossing bank, only two vehicles moved on Main Street. A 4010 John Deere tractor was headed west, pulling an empty wagon, while eighty-six-year-old Shank Williams piloted his vintage car east.

The temperature-time sign suspended from the bank flashed two forty-five. She'd made it in time to make her deposit, she thought with a sigh. As she switched off the pickup, the sign changed to flash fifty-two degrees, which was warm for mid-March in northwestern Iowa.

Irene Sparks, proprietress of Irene's Café, came from the bank and, seeing Meghan in the pickup, smiled and waved. Meghan returned the cordial gesture, then watched as the plump, middle-aged woman walked down the block toward her café, located on the corner.

Meghan reflected she couldn't have purchased a veterinarian practice in a friendlier community. She amended her thought when Irene stopped in front of Diller's grocery store to talk to a blond, bearded man.

The man engaged in lively conversation with Irene was an exception to the rule, at least where Meghan was concerned. Yesterday though he'd physically run into her at Diller's, he hadn't introduced himself. He'd barely apologized for shoving her nose-first into the chest-type vegetable freezer.

So...he hadn't exactly run into her, nor had he reached out with menace to shove her. But it *was* because of him that she'd taken the undignified plunge into the freezer. She supposed the whole thing could have been avoided if she hadn't been so preoccupied with trying to decide what to have for supper.

Meghan hated cooking, so whatever vegetable she chose would constitute the main course of her meal that day. Since Diller's had been low on stock, she'd been bent over and deep into the freezer. She remembered thinking she'd go with mixed vegetables, if she could only find them. She'd heard a steely bang and her cart, which had been standing in the aisle behind her, had hit her in the posterior. She'd pitched forward, her fingers splaying on packages of frozen vegetables.

"Oops! Sorry!" a tenor voice had mumbled.

Meghan had come up fuming, sure she'd heard laughter in the apology. But by the time she'd regained her footing, the blond man had sped with his cart to the checkout counter.

Meghan shifted in the seat now, glancing into the rearview mirror to check her hair. She fluffed the red strands by running her fingers through it. When she straightened in the seat and looked back up the sidewalk, she discovered Mr. Notable Exception striding in her direction.

* * *

As soon as Thane MacDougal left Irene to head for the bank, he saw the new vet, Meghan Forester, sitting in her fiery red pickup. He had to admit he was curious about the woman who'd purchased Doc Ableson's clinic and practice when the old man had retired. He'd been curious ever since Tina Greer, Megan Forester's secretary, had put the bug in his ear.

"In case you haven't heard," Tina had said, her eyes bright with matchmaker enthusiasm, "Meghan is a redhead. About thirty. And she's eligible."

Tina and her husband, Bill, had grown up with Thane and were his closest friends. The three had remained close even when Thane had left Beaver Crossing for college at Iowa State and later had lived in Dallas, Texas, during his marriage. He knew it was in the name of friendship that Tina had informed him the vet was eligible and suggested supper at the Greers some night so that he and Meghan could meet socially.

Thane had bluntly informed Tina that he wasn't interested in meeting the vet in any way but professionally, which was inevitable; he raised hogs and had a small cow and calf operation, and she was the only vet in town.

But personally he wasn't interested. Burned once by a woman whose ambition had caused her to devote more time to her career than to their marriage, he wasn't about to cuddle up to the same kind of bonfire. No matter how attractive the fire...

Meghan couldn't take her gaze off the man walking toward her. It wasn't that she was interested in him in any way but professionally. It was just that with his striking golden hair and tawny beard he would have stood out on a crowded city street, so it was entirely understandable, Meghan thought, that she would notice him here in Beaver Crossing, population 503. She would have to be wearing blinders not to. In the month she'd been in town, she'd noticed the man, say, half a dozen times. Say, *exactly* six times if she counted today, she admitted ruefully.

Long legs, confident stride. Mid-thirties, she decided as the gap between her and the blond man narrowed. He passed the empty lot between the drug store and the bank building. In the mid-afternoon sun his body cast a long shadow, while golden-white highlights rippled through his hair. What need would a man have for such beautiful hair? Meghan was thinking when he stopped not ten feet away, looked directly at her and caught her staring.

Meghan's first impulse was to feign a swoon and slide out of sight behind the dashboard. Imagine! she scoffed at herself. Someone her age getting caught gawking. What a predicament: she'd never developed a convincing swoon. Instead, she blushed an unflattering shade of pink while her lips curved in a stupid grin.

In response, the man tossed her a brusque nod and an equally abrupt wave. Meghan tilted her head in acknowledgment, and he scowled, wheeled and entered the bank.

"Be jiggered," Meghan muttered. Now, *that* was plain rude! And she knew she hadn't imagined it. While his gestures had been hurried, his gaze on her hadn't been. He had taken an in-depth inventory before dismissing her as if she wore a wart on her nose. She tapped the end of her nose. It *did* do kind of a little flip on the end, but she hadn't sprouted a wart.

Frowning, she took her billfold from the glove compartment, opened the cab door, swung her jeans-covered legs from the cab and stepped to the pavement. She wasn't accustomed to anyone not smiling at her... especially not after she'd smiled first—even if it had been a foolish grin. The point was she had smiled and she had expected a smile in return.

Heck. He probably wasn't worth being curious about, she told herself. He probably was married. And if he wasn't, it was because no sensible woman would have him. He would dislike children; loathe cats and dogs and buttered pop-corn. No doubt about it, he was positively un-American.

Chapter One

As Meghan tucked her billfold into her jacket pocket she glanced up at the bank clock again. Two forty-eight. She'd have to do an imitation of a hurricane in order to get back to the clinic before Tina left for her dentist appointment at three.

Some days Meghan found herself constantly checking the time, chasing herself and never catching up. Today had been like that, wild and chaotic. She'd been behind schedule from the moment the alarm had rung, at six-thirty. But she wouldn't complain about her life. The trade-off for her hectic pace was professional accomplishment.

Meghan had shut the pickup door and was stepping onto the sidewalk when her attention was drawn up the street by a man yelling, "Watch it, Shank!" She looked in time to catch Shank completing an illegal U-turn in the intersection. Judging by the reaction of the tractor driver who had shouted, she guessed that Shank had made his move without giving any indication of his intent.

Meanwhile Shank, oblivious to the shouting, piloted his car west, toward Meghan. Shaking her head, Meghan stepped to the bank door and grimaced when she heard the squeak of brakes. Oh, land, she thought, was Shank going to park? Next to her pickup? She hated to look, but couldn't resist.

Shank was parking, aiming at a space between her pickup and a relic of one that had more rust showing than faded blue paint. He missed her tailgate by six inches, which Meghan suspected he would consider was as good as a mile, then inched forward.

When the right front tire of the car bounced on the curb, Shank shifted into neutral, rolled the window down and craned his weathered neck out. "Thought I was goin' to nick yer car, didn't ya?"

"Shank, that was not a *car* you missed but my pickup," Meghan said, correcting him on his slight oversight.

Shank squinted behind thick-lensed glasses. "Hell! Hi ya, Doc. Didn't know it was you standin' there till you started talkin'. Thought you was Etta Parker. Pulled in to see how she's doin' since she got her gallbladder out. What else I miss besides your pickup?" he asked. Raising his voice a notch because the tractor was passing on the street behind him, he answered himself. "She-ute. It's Thane Mac-Dougal's pickup. Good thing I didn't clip 'er. Thane's awful particular when it comes to that pickup o' his. Treats her near as good as he does the Bateman woman he's been courtin'."

Thane MacDougal? The name didn't ring a bell. And while Meghan knew Shank was known as much for stretching the truth as he was for his wacky driving, if this Thane MacDougal treated the rusty relic the way he treated his woman friend, the woman must be suffering a sad state of neglect.

"What are you up to, Shank?" Meghan asked.

"I'm too dang old to be up to much, but I hear you were out at Peterson's place yesterday, dehornin'. Matt says you did a good job. Better than he expected, you bein' no heavyweight."

"Sometimes a job requires more finesse than brute strength," Meghan offered with a smile.

Shank laughed. "If finesse means havin' pretty red hair and big blue eyes, then I guess you know what you're talkin' about."

"I like to think that I know what I'm talking about."

"Let me tell you somethin', Doc," Shank said. "When you get right down to the nubbin', talkin' isn't near as important as doin', and I hear you're doin' okay. A real go-getter. An' speakin' of goin', I got to be. If I don't get home pretty soon, Amy Lou'll be thinkin' I went 'n' had an accident. Dang woman. After sixty-five years of bein' married to me, she ain't learned yet I can drive a car by myself. She thinks I need a keeper."

"Hate to tell you, Shank," Megan said. "But when it comes to driving, Amy Lou's right. You do need a keeper."

Shank snorted a laugh.

Meghan grinned. "Tell Amy Lou hello for me."

"Sure thing." Shank gunned the car's idling motor, which misfired as he shifted into reverse.

Meghan half turned, reaching for the handle of the bank door. The next thing she knew she was thrown backward, her arms flailing as a resonant tenor voice roared in her ear, "Shank! Crank her left! You're going to scrape Blythe's running board!"

Meghan, blindly reaching for something to grab, latched on to the lapels of the blond man's jacket. In stumbling backward, she jerked so hard on the material that the action threatened to put them in a pile.

His hands flew out to grab her forearms. Meghan felt the strength of his fingers through the thick lining of her jacket

before he drew her toward him into something that reminded her very much of an embrace. Yet his eyes were focused somewhere over her shoulder. Meghan's gaze followed
his. Shank was waving as he drove away, blissfully unaware
of the havoc he'd caused.

When Meghan looked back, she discovered herself peering into incredibly distinctive, beautiful eyes. Were they pecan-colored? Or were they what they appeared to be...sun-
colored? Couldn't be yellow. Yellow was genetically impossible. Wasn't it? Ten years of studying one science or
another and she was drawing a blank.

Up close, Thane saw that the fire of Meghan Forester's
hair was russet. Its silver fingers framed a face that was
more oval than round. Her surprise at finding herself in his
arms was reflected in the blue-black ink of her eyes. The vet
wears perfume? he thought as the scent swirled around him,
bringing to his nostrils the smell of spring after a rain.

Feeling bumbling and inarticulate, he said, "Excuse me.
I didn't see you standing there when I shoved the door open.
All I saw was Shank about to take out my pickup."

Meghan tried to sort out the wild thoughts rushing
through her mind. So this was Thane MacDougal. Full
golden brows. Nice nose. High, strong cheekbones. Beard
trimmed, silky-looking—but wait a darn minute! This was
the man who not five minutes ago had been downright rude.

"I think your concern about the pickup was unwar-
ranted, Mr. MacDougal. Shank knew you'd be upset with
him if he clipped it," she said.

"Did I detect a trace of sarcasm in your voice when you
referred to Blythe as an *it*?" Thane asked, pretending to be
offended.

Meghan pursed her lips in concentration. Was that a smile
she detected hiding on his lips, a dimple hidden in his beard?
"Blythe is a pretty fancy handle for a pickup, isn't it?"

"Actually, Blythe was my dad's pickup," Thane said. "After he died, I kept calling her Blythe because she seems like a Blythe to me. I know she looks a bit worse for wear, body wise, but it's what's under the hood that counts, isn't it?"

"You're right," Meghan said, scolding herself for reading innuendo into an innocent conversation. "What's important is how the pickup runs. Not how it looks."

She was being so...dumb, Meghan thought. He couldn't help what seemed to be an intense study of her. He'd been born with the rays of the sun in his eyes, intense and burning. But because of that intensity she felt weak-kneed, and he was still holding her. "Uh . . . you can let go of me," she said.

Thane's gaze dropped to where his fingers were wrapped lightly around her forearms. His rapt attention had been on her face, and he hadn't realized he still held her arms. His gaze was drawn back to her lovely face, which was still worthy of attention, he found himself thinking.

"You're sure I didn't knock the wind out of you? You appear wobbly to me," he said. Despite the air of desperation he could hear in his voice, he thought his excuse for still holding her sounded feasible.

"Wobbly? Nonsense," Meghan said, denying her self-evaluation of the effect his eyes had on her. "I'm fine. You can let me go."

Thane didn't want to release her. He'd felt softness where he'd expected steel, smelled sweetness when he'd anticipated sour. No, he didn't want to free her, but he lifted his hands from her arms.

Just as he moved left, she moved right.

"Excuse me again," Thane said. They were eye to eye and nose to nose. He saw that her nose turned up on the end and had a smattering of freckles across the bridge that some-

how made her approachable—if he'd wanted to approach
her, which of course he did not.

Touch me. She'll laugh.

That was the tip of her nose teasing Thane. His smile
came from a blend of amusement and self-derision. Sane
thoughts had scampered from his mind like field mice skit-
tering to safety from a nest unearthed by a plow. What he
was left with was almost an edict: touch the tip of her nose.

"I . . . have to be going," Meghan murmured, stepping to
the right, only to discover he'd chosen that moment to move
left. They were nose to nose again.

"Da—cockroaches," she said, flushing in embarrassment. His lips when he grinned were a shade too wide, but
full. Kissable. She'd never kissed a man with a beard, she
mused.

"'Cockroaches' instead of profanity?" Thane asked.

Meghan could only smile foolishly. "Listen," she said.
"Since we don't seem to be making much progress, I propose you stay where you are and I'll move around you."

"You think if you can get me to remain stationary you'll
have a good chance of getting around me?" Thane asked.
The words came by rote, because he wasn't here; he was
there . . . lost in the depths of her inky eyes. . . .

Meghan cleared her throat. She was going to say something, but he had her so distracted. What had he asked? Oh,
yes. "I may not have a good chance of getting around you,
but I will have a better chance if you stay where you are,"
she said lightly.

"You're that eager to go, Dr. Forester?"

"Eager to go, Mr. MacDougal?" Meghan questioned
with a trace of irony, recalling how he'd left Diller's grocery store while she was still digging herself out of the
freezer. If *his* exit hadn't been eager, she didn't know the
meaning of the word.

"Please, call me Thane," he requested. "I imagine we'll be bumping into each other from time to time."

"Haven't you bumped into me before today?" she asked slowly, making her expression unreadable. "Or do you have a twin running around Beaver Crossing pushing a grocery cart?"

"No twin. But I didn't bump you. The cart you were using nudged you," Thane said.

"I *know* what hit me," Meghan said. From the merriment showing in his eyes she knew that he'd been laughing as he'd made his escape.

"*Nudged*. As in gentle bump," Thane said, emphasizing the *bump*. "Admit it, Meghan. You were already standing on your head in that freezer when I arrived on the scene. Surprise caused you to lose your balance."

Meghan thought the sound of her name coming from his lips was lovely, and the exquisite smile in his eyes was asking her to laugh. But, darn it, she was not going to laugh, because even though he was right, it was the principle of the thing, the indignity of it. She was *not* going to respond to his teasing, she was telling herself when she broke up—giggling first, then laughing.

Thane leaned against the brick wall of the bank, watching Meghan. She had every right to be angry, but somehow he'd known she'd laugh. What he hadn't guessed was how deep-throated and body-involving her laughter would be, how his heart would begin to race.

When she'd quieted, he said, "I apologize for my behavior yesterday. I should have stopped, introduced myself and welcomed you to Beaver Crossing."

"Why didn't you?" Meghan asked. Simultaneously the answer hit her. "I understand! Shank said—oh, my. You're engaged or something, aren't you?"

Scandalized by her outburst, she went pink. She'd sounded like a barker for a sideshow. She retreated a step. "I'm sorry! I can't believe I said that, so pinch me."

Thane extended his fingers to apply tender pressure just under the point of her chin, then when she didn't jump away screaming for the law but only stood there, waiting for his next move, he trailed his fingers down the soft skin of her neck to the collar of her jacket before he dropped his hand.

"I didn't mean pinch me—literally," Meghan whispered. She was reeling from his touch on her chin? Impossible!

"Shank talks too much sometimes." Thane forced the words around a tightness in his throat. Static electricity from the dry air, he assured himself. That accounted for the sparks he'd felt in his fingertips when he touched her. "I'm not engaged...or something. I didn't hurt you when I pinched you, did I?"

"No, you only surprised me," Meghan said.

Thane reminded himself to deal with Meghan Forester on a detached, unemotional basis. But he saw how she tilted her head as she listened to him, saw how her eyes half closed when she was considering what he'd said, felt how he warmed when her gaze locked on his. There was no coyness about her; she liked what she saw in him and allowed him to see it.

"I'm surprising myself," he admitted. "Would you like to join me at Irene's for a cup of coffee?"

"Right now?" Megan wasn't nearly as shocked by his asking as she was baffled by how badly she wanted to go with him.

"I'd thought now—if you aren't busy."

"That's the problem. I can't right now. I'm running behind schedule." Hoping he would suggest another time, she allowed her disappointment to sound in her voice.

The romantic bubble Thane had been riding burst with a resounding bang. She was running behind schedule. How many times had he heard that one before? With his ex-wife it had meant she was late for an appointment with a client; with Meghan it would mean she was late for a date with some steer or sow.

"Fine," Thane said, terse. "I understand."

"I'm sorry, Thane. Couldn't we make it another time?" Meghan asked despite the warning flag he'd raised. And the fact that he was evasive now about looking her in the eye.

"Sure. Some other time." He forced himself to look into her eyes again and tried to appear amicable, though he was a little irritated at himself for giving in to the impulse to ask her for coffee.

Meghan realized there was no real warmth in his smile. In a flash he'd gone from genial and spontaneous to distant and cold. "You don't intend to make it another time, do you?"

"I doubt it," Thane admitted.

"I don't understand," Meghan said, perplexed.

Thane heaved a sigh of resignation. He owed her an explanation. "I was married once. I played second fiddle to the woman's career and didn't like it. I forgot for a minute how much I didn't like it—until you reminded me by saying you were running behind schedule."

"I see," Meghan said. "Only non-career types are eligible to have coffee with you."

"I don't want hard feelings between us, Meghan," Thane said, knowing whatever he said wouldn't soothe the scorching anger he saw in her eyes.

"I don't have hard feelings for you." She wanted to plant her fist on the end of his nose. But she wasn't going to give Thane MacDougal the satisfaction of knowing he'd touched her emotionally. She smiled. "See you around, MacDougal."

The sweet smile didn't fool Thane. It was dripping with ridicule. He'd accomplished one thing. He wouldn't have to avoid Meghan Forester to avoid testing himself. When she saw him coming she'd take flight like a pheasant at the sound of a gun blast.

"Sure," he said. "See you around. I farm east of town. Raise hogs and a few cattle. I need a vet occasionally."

Meghan laughed—a little wildly, she realized. He'd wanted to get better acquainted until she'd reminded him of what she did for a living. Now he'd call her when he needed a vet?

"Keep me in mind," she said.

She walked away, thinking how close she'd come to making a fool of herself. Close? Capital letters: MEGHAN ACTED LIKE A FOOL. And over a man whose perception of women was myopic. Well, she was back in control now. No more banging heart or misty vision that made the man appear bigger than life.

Oh, no! She was at Diller's grocery store, and she'd been going into the bank. Having gotten groceries only yesterday, she needed nothing in Diller's. But she would think of something to buy. Cheese, maybe. Anything to justify stopping at the store. She would *not* have Thane Mac-Dougal witness her in an about-face.

Thane stayed where he was when Meghan walked away. He'd made a fool of himself, he thought, recalling those few minutes when his body had betrayed his mind. But he was back in the here and now and focused on reality.

Meghan was lovely to look at. But it ended there, because if there was a next time for him, it was going to be the right kind of woman, a him-oriented woman. If that made him a chauvinist, well, so be it.

A veterinarian who smelled of the promise of spring, whose eyes made sensual promises, whose russet hair begged

fingering and whose pixie nose begged touching was still a
veterinarian. She didn't have time for a lover, let alone a
family. She'd likely decided this for herself, he realized.
With all she had going for her, why else would she be sin-
gle?

He shook his head in bemusement. With most women he
was stoic, keeping his romantic-impulsive self under control. Yet with Meghan he'd sounded as if he were partici-
pating in a contest for palaverer of the year. What he'd been
was pathetic.

He dreaded facing her again.

Meghan rushed through her "grocery" shopping. Not
wanting to chance a second confrontation with Mac-
Dougal, she skipped going into the bank to make her deposit. Still, she arrived at the clinic to find she'd missed
Tina.

She placed her package on the desk and picked up the
notepad to read the notations Tina'd left her.

Boss lady. One feline patient admitted this afternoon.
Finnigin is caged in the kennel. Needs a distemper shot.
Murphy will pick up his kitten after school, sometime
around 3:45. Please tell him to wait here for his dad to
come for him and not go wandering around town.

If Chip happens to be with Murphy, instead of at
Marlene's for his piano lesson, remind that kid of mine
where he's supposed to be.

William Walkerman called wondering if he should
vaccinate his gilts with five-way lepto, parvo, erysipe-
las and pseudorabies. You're to call him.

And your mother called. She wanted to know if
you'd broken both arms, since you'd neither called nor
written in a month. I assured her both arms were in
mint condition. She concluded you were a negligent

daughter. I had to agree.

Meghan thought, Thanks heaps, Tina, then continued
reading.

Your mother asked if there were any eligible men in
Beaver Crossing. I gave her a listing of them. She asked
if you'd shown interest in any particular man.

Meghan paused, shaking her head. Her mother was an
incurable romantic. It wasn't that Meghan didn't believe in
romantic love. But that misty-minded state always happened to other women, like her sister, Sue. Or Tina.
In fact, Meghan had begun to wonder if she appealed to
men in a romantic light. MacDougal? That wasn't romantic appeal. That was basic male-female attraction—although, she thought, for a few minutes it had seemed
there'd been the potential for more.

I haven't forgotten you wanted to inventory and order
tomorrow morning. I'll be here by eight. Tina.

Meghan thought fondly how glad she was that she'd
found Tina. Tina had worked for Dr. Ableson and had
agreed to stay on after Meghan took over the business. The
two women had quickly developed a sisterly relationship, a
blend of combative affection and candor. Meghan's back-
yard and that of Tina and Bill Greer met at the alley.
Meghan often opened her back door in answer to a knock
to happily discover that ten-year-old Chip or four-year-old
Nance Greer had come for a visit. Thinking of Chip reminded Meghan of the kitten waiting in the kennel.
She broke off her thoughts to glance at the clock. School
had been dismissed five minutes ago. She left her desk,
crossed the reception room and entered a long hall. When

she reached the kennel, she hung up her jacket and moved to the cage where Finnigin was being held.

"Hello, there," she crooned to the kitten, which had un-curled from a sleeping ball and was stretching. Meghan un-locked the cage, opened the door and took the kitten into her arms.

"Poor baby. In a strange place all by yourself. Let's get this distemper shot over with, shall we?"

She ran her fingers through the kitten's coat. Soft as silk, Meghan was reflecting when she realized she wasn't think-ing about the kitten's fur but Thane MacDougal's beard.

Not to mention his pecan-colored eyes, his teasing and tempting smile, she thought as she carried the kitten from the kennel to the adjacent examining room. She had to ad-mit she'd found Thane MacDougal interesting, despite the confusing signals he'd given her. His smile said, *I trust you. Approach me.* The tension lines that had developed around his eyes told her he didn't trust her, and his words ex-pressed his wish that she'd keep her distance.

She set the kitten on the examining table, announcing, "So much for Thane MacDougal."

Chapter Two

In a minute Meghan had prepared the syringe and vaccine. The kitten was in excellent condition, though there had apparently been a case of mistaken identity. A Finnigin she wasn't. Fifi or Fidelia, maybe.

Meghan administered the shot, then set the syringe aside. Gathering the kitten into her arms, she turned toward the open door of the examining room to greet the visitor she sensed had been watching her.

The boy standing in the doorway was slightly built and had an unruly crop of red hair. His nose and cheekbones were angular and covered with freckles. The green-eyed gaze meeting Meghan's was shy and serious.

"Murphy, I presume," she said.

He nodded, stuck his hands into the pockets of his denim jacket as he edged his way into the room. All four feet six inches of him was trying to be nonchalant, while the shuffling of his feet on the rough board of the floor told Meghan he wasn't.

"I think Finnigin is happy the distemper shot is over," Meghan said.

A smile, albeit a tentative one, developed in Murphy's eyes as he spoke. "I don't think Finnigin even felt the shot. It was neat, the way you did it, Dr. Forester."

"Thank you, Murphy. But would you please call me Doc or Meghan?" she suggested.

"I'll call you Doc." A full-blown smile surfaced on the boy's face.

Meghan reciprocated, and for a moment they stood in open admiration of each other before she said, "I gather from a note Tina left me that you and Chip are friends. Did he go for his piano lesson?" The kitten stretched and craned her neck to look at her owner. Meghan extended the kitten to Murphy.

The hands that came from Murphy's pockets to accept the kitten were long-fingered and slightly grubby. "Chip's taking his piano lesson, all right, 'cause his dad told him that if he *forgot* his lesson again, he'd get grounded for a year."

"I can see from the twinkle in your eyes that you don't think Mr. Greer would do that to Chip," Meghan stated.

A waggish expression came to Murphy's face. "Nope. Mr. Greer only talks tough. A month maybe—tops."

Meghan laughed. She agreed with Murphy's assessment of Bill. If there was a disciplinarian in the Greer family, it was Tina. She noticed that Murphy's eyes widened as if he were surprised he'd made her laugh. Meghan felt a familiar longing—the longing to have a child.

When she realized her sober scrutiny was making Murphy uncomfortable, she asked, "Has Finnigin been wormed?"

"Not yet."

"Then I'll give you a pill to take home. Give it in the morning before you feed and water. Do you know how to get Finnigin's mouth open?"

Murphy placed his thumb and index finger at the hinge of Finnigin's jaw and applied slight pressure. The kitten's mouth opened. Murphy looked up, asking, "Now what?"

"Once Finnigin's mouth is open, place the pill on the back of the tongue. Close the mouth. Hold it closed and rub the throat like this," Meghan said, bending to demonstrate the procedure.

"The pill won't choke Finnigin?" Murphy asked, worried.

"No," Meghan assured him, then patted Finnigin's head and stepped back.

He took his fingers from the kitten's jaws, then looked up at Meghan, consternation still on his face. "I don't know if I have enough hands to open Finnigin's mouth, stick the pill in, close it and stroke."

"Maybe your father or mother can help you."

"There's just Dad. My mother and Dad got divorced six years ago, when we came back to Iowa to farm the home place after Grandpa got sick." He gazed around the room, taking a quick inventory, then looked back at Meghan. "My mother, Cassandra, lives in Dallas, but she travels a lot— she's a corporate lawyer."

Murphy's voice had been steady and lacking emotion, but Meghan could see a quandary of emotion reflected in his eyes. "Being a lawyer sounds exciting," she offered.

Murphy, gnawing on the inside of his lip, wandered across the room to the kennel door. He glanced into the kennel, then back at Meghan, who was leaning against the examining table.

"My mother says being a lawyer is the greatest thing that ever happened to her," he said slowly. Then his words came in a rush. "I don't see her much. Sometimes . . . it's like she doesn't want me with her. And then I get to thinking Cassandra doesn't like me much."

"I'm sure that isn't true." Meghan offered the rebuttal softly. She was jarred by Murphy's referring to his mother as Cassandra.

"That's what Dad says. He says my mother likes me okay. It's just hard for her to have me around when she's working. But I'm going to be eleven on May eighteenth, so I'm old enough to know whether someone likes me or not."

Meghan's heart twisted. Her urge was to step to Murphy, gather him to her and hug him to assure him that someone loved him. She sensed, however, that he might misconstrue the gesture, think she was feeling sorry for him.

"It sounds as if you and your father get along pretty well," she ventured.

"Yes. We do," Murphy agreed, brightening. "Course, sometimes he yells at me when I forget to shut a pasture gate or leave the farrowing-house door open."

Meghan picked up the disposable syringe she'd used on Finnigin and threw it away.

"Dads can be awfully narrow-minded about gates left open, can't they?" she said, giving Murphy a deadpan look. He understood the jest and snickered. "And speaking of Dads. Tina said your father would pick you up here, so why don't we have a visit until he comes?"

Meghan gestured to a chair. He crossed the room and sat, while she positioned herself on a stool.

After Murphy had settled Finnigin on his lap, he looked at Meghan, open in his scrutiny. "Chip says you aren't married."

"No. I'm not married."

"And you don't have any kids," Murphy stated.

"Chip said?"

"Yeah. Chip told me you don't have kids. Would you like some?"

"I'd love to have children," Meghan said, bantering. "You know how it is—your dad has you to help with chores around the farm, but I don't have anyone to help out around here. Clean cages and sweep floors, that kind of thing." To make sure Murphy understood that she was playing, she grinned.

Murphy gave grin for grin, and the air seemed to charge with excitement. Meghan reflected that Murphy was charming. The beauty of it was he didn't know it.

"So you're looking for one?" Murphy said.

"I'm sorry, Murphy. You lost me. Am I looking for one what?"

Murphy cocked his head, eyeing her in a definitely condescending manner. "A husband. You can't have kids unless you have a husband. So you're looking for one, right?"

Meghan unglued her tongue from where it had plastered on her teeth. "Well...you do have a point. But I'm not really *looking* for a husband, Murphy. All I can say is that I'd think about getting married if the right man came along."

"Wow!" Murphy punctuated his exclamation by pointing his right index finger into the air in front of him. "Do you know my dad says the same thing? He'd think about getting married if the right woman came along."

Murphy's eyes slitted and his lashes fluttered, and Meghan realized that his innocence was a guise. The little devil had managed a neat bit of subterfuge.

"You aren't thinking of playing matchmaker for your father and me, are you, Murphy?"

"That's what I was thinking," he admitted gleefully.

"What would your father say if he knew what you're trying to do?"

"He'd be madder than heck at first," Murphy said, unconcerned. "But he'd settle down once he got used to the idea."

"Would he, now?" Meghan asked as she pushed herself from the stool. "Before I forget, I'd better get Finnigin's pill. Be back in a minute."

Once she was out of Murphy's sight and hearing, she chuckled. His father would settle down once he got used to the idea. She shook her head and laughed again. It would be a safe bet that life with Murphy would never be dull.

As she opened the storage-room refrigerator, her brow furrowed in thought. She was bothered by those flashes of bewildered sadness she'd witnessed in Murphy's eyes when he talked about his mother.

Yet whatever the circumstances of his parents' divorce, and no matter whether Murphy was right about his mother's feeling toward him, one thing was clear: his father had tried to allay Murphy's fear that his mother didn't love him. The man apparently knew he'd get no personal satisfaction from reinforcing Murphy's belief that his mother didn't love him. Murphy's father must be a sensitive person.

When Meghan stepped back into the examining room, Murphy exploded with conversation even while she stuffed into his jacket pocket a small envelope containing the pill and instructions.

"You know, I could help you clean cages and sweep floors," he remarked.

Murphy was smiling, but Meghan saw a hint of questioning in his eyes. Was he testing her, seeing if she would refuse and so be like the mother he thought didn't want him around?

"I'd like to have you help me, Murphy. Anytime you can."

"I could come Monday afternoon after school for a while. Dad's got a parent-teacher conference. I was going home with Chip, but I could come here instead."

"Fine by me," Meghan said. "If it's okay with your father, we've got a date—Monday after school."

She reached down, removed Murphy's cap, smoothed his hair, then replaced the cap at the same angle. "I've been wondering why you call your kitten Finnigin."

"Why'd you do that?" he asked.

"Straighten your hair?"

Murphy, looking up at her from under the bill of the cap, nodded.

She didn't know how to answer. He'd looked as if he needed touching? She'd felt a need to touch him? "Don't know. Just did. Shouldn't I have?"

"It's okay. I kinda liked it. I'll bet you think I don't know Finnigin is a female," he said, answering Meghan's original question.

"That's what I thought." Meghan returned to the stool.

"Heck. I know one gender from another—Dad taught me." Murphy moved his fingers over the kitten, stroking it head to tail. "I found her one day in a snowdrift when she wasn't old enough to be weaned. Don't know how she got there, but I suppose her mom was carrying her and forgot where she dropped her. Anyway, I looked down and there she was, stiff as a board, so I took her into the house."

Meghan nodded, listening.

Murphy continued his story. "Dad said to me, 'It doesn't look good for her, Murphy.'" He looked up at Meghan. "That was because she was stiff and all. But Dad said we'd give a try at saving her, so he got the hair dryer and we used it to dry her off. Then we wrapped her in a towel and stuck her in the oven at one hundred degrees with the door open because—" Murphy paused for dramatic effect "—Dad said we wanted *warmed* cat, not baked cat."

"You bet," Meghan said. "Wouldn't want baked cat—yuk!" She made an awful face by screwing up her nose and lips.

Murphy's laugh rocked his body. "Man, Doc. You're fun."

Meghan chuckled along with him while wondering what caused Murphy to say she was fun. Hadn't he had fun with his mother? She knew Murphy had fun with his father. Only a man with a sense of humor would tell his son that they wanted warmed cat, not baked cat. Yet by telling him that it didn't look good for the kitten, he'd also prepared Murphy for the possibility Finnigin could die.

The more Murphy revealed about his father, the more Meghan found herself thinking the man was someone she would like to know. Maybe being introduced to him wasn't such an outlandish idea. Or was she thinking that because she was looking at the red-haired Murphy and seeing in him the child she'd always wanted? she mused.

Meghan was so lost in thought that she hadn't realized Murphy had left the chair and crossed the room until he was standing before her.

"I'm to the part now about how Finnigan got her name, but I've got to show you," Murphy explained. He rubbed the kitten under its chin. Finnigin's eyes closed, and her white whiskers came forward in response. "Some set of whiskers, isn't it?" he asked proudly.

"I've never seen a kitten with longer whiskers. That's for sure," Meghan said.

"I measured her whiskers," he said. "Two-and-one-half inches long. Now my dad always sings this song called 'Michael Finnigin,' because he has whiskers on his chin just like the song says Finnigin does. You ever heard of it, Doc?"

Meghan broke into a lively rendition of "Michael Finnigin." Before the chorus, Murphy was singing along. They were hot into the third verse and rollicking when a melodious tenor voice joined Meghan's alto and Murphy's soprano.

Meghan looked to the door and bolted from the stool. She was barely able to keep the smile on her face, the lilt in her voice. She should have known: Thane MacDougal.

When the song was done, Murphy said, "Doc wanted to know how Finnigin got her name, Dad."

Thane stepped into the room. "I suppose you gave her every detail," he said, waiting for his son to look at him, waiting for Meghan to look at him. But Murphy was smiling at Meghan. And Meghan was smiling at Murphy. And it was their smiles, Murphy's glowing and Meghan's hauntingly beautiful, that made him wonder how she'd won his son's trust so quickly and completely.

"You have a delightful son, Thane," Meghan said when she found the courage to meet his gaze fully.

"I didn't know you knew my dad," Murphy said.

"We met earlier this afternoon, but I didn't know until now that he was your father," Megan replied.

"Say, Dad!" Murphy exploded. "Since tomorrow is Saturday, how about asking Doc out to our place for supper?"

Thane studied Murphy's expectant expression. Supper? Tomorrow night? Yes. He'd heard the question correctly. The problem was how he could say no to Murphy without sounding as if he were saying no.

Meghan was about to refuse the invitation when she saw that Thane had no intention of allowing it to stand but was trying to think of a way to worm out of it.

That threw a new light on the polite refusal she'd been about to offer. So what if she was an ineligible, she thought. She'd be darned if she'd help MacDougal squirm out of the hole Murphy had dug for him.

"I think it will have to be some other time, Murphy," Thane said.

"Some other time?" Murphy questioned. Thane tried his reliable knock-it-off-kid look, which Murphy ignored by asking, "Why?"

Thane entrenched, taking the firm-tone tack. "We're having supper at Betty Bateman's."

"Again!" Murphy lamented.

Thane reddened. He couldn't believe Murphy was doing this to him. It was bad enough he'd made a fool of himself in front of Meghan *once* today, and now this. More firmly he said, "Yes, Murphy. Again!"

Meghan was getting nearly perverse pleasure from witnessing Thane's discomfiture. Hadn't he told her he wasn't engaged... or something? But he was having supper with Betty again. Thane glanced at her, catching her midstream in petty thought. She feigned disinterest in Thane's exchange with Murphy.

Thane shifted uneasily under the onslaught of the accusation of unfairness in Murphy's gaze. "Well," he said in a cheery tone. "Chore time, Murphy. We've got to be going. Meghan, how much do I owe you?"

"We owe for a worm pill, too," Murphy said. "I've got it in my pocket."

"Three dollars," Meghan said when Thane's gaze shifted from Murphy to her.

Thane took out his billfold, counted the bills out and extended them toward Meghan.

Meghan reached to receive them.

Their fingers brushed. Their gazes met and locked.

Static electricity, hell, Thane was thinking as he snatched his fingers back.

Meghan thought, How unfair of him to judge all career women because of a bad experience with one. Well, she didn't care how narrow-minded the man was. She didn't want any more contact with him than was necessary.

Thane and Meghan disengaged their gazes, each believing they had eliminated any possibility of further encounters of a personal nature.

Thane slipped his billfold back into his pocket, placed his hands on Murphy's shoulders and wheeled him toward the door.

"Guess we're leaving, Doc," Murphy said as his father guided him through the door and up the hall. "Thanks for everything. See you Monday after school, okay?"

Meghan followed them into the hall. "Okay."

"What's this about Monday after school?" Thane asked.

Murphy stalled, looking up and over his shoulder at his father. "I was going to tell you, Dad," he said. "Doc asked me to help her clean cages while you were at the parent-teacher conference. I can, can't I?"

Frowning, Thane touched Murphy lightly on the shoulder to urge him to keep walking. Thane glanced back at Meghan. "Did you ask him?"

Why, he can be as growly as an old bear, Meghan reflected. She wanted to tell him that frowning didn't become him. "I invited Murphy to visit anytime he wanted," she said.

Murphy spoke up. "See, Dad? I can come *anytime*."

Thane nudged him forward into the reception room. "Okay, Murphy," he said, sounding gruff. "But don't make a pest of yourself."

"See you Monday, Doc."

"Bye, Murphy. See you Monday," Meghan said. She shot a daggered gaze at Thane's back. Had he really called his son a pest? The only pest in the MacDougal clan came with a tawny beard. But she wouldn't stoop to his level of rudeness by telling him he was rude. She'd fight his rudeness with sweetness.

"Bye, Thane," she said with all the saccharine she could muster. In fact, she sounded so unlike herself she almost lost it and laughed.

Thane wanted to be furious with Meghan. He'd seen how she'd pretended indifference to the supper invitation while her eyes had revealed she'd enjoyed every blessed moment he had spent squirming out of it. But the faked sweetness in her voice was so outrageous that his inclination was to laugh with her at himself—something he hadn't done in a long time.

He glanced over his shoulder. "Bye, Meghan," he said, putting as much syrup in his voice as she had.

Murphy asked, "Something wrong, Dad? You sound funny."

"Move it," Thane said, no longer nudging but marching Murphy across the reception room toward the door.

Meghan entered the reception room, then stood for a moment reflecting that though Thane hadn't laughed, he had smiled. And what a smile! It was warming and wonderful, an all-is-right-with-the-world kind of smile, and Meghan felt its absence after he'd turned away.

Then they were gone.

Meghan walked to the window and watched as Thane backed Blythe from the curb. Murphy waved. Meghan waved and remained at the window until the truck was out of sight, then turned, glancing around the room, to wall shelves filled with medical and stock supplies, to the stacks of sacks holding calf and lamb milk replacer, to Tina's desk, to the free-standing shelves and finally to the glass-topped counter that held the cash register.

These were the token symbols indicating she'd arrived at an important objective in her professional career, she reflected. But for the first time since she'd purchased the clinic, she felt something other than pride in ownership. She felt loneliness, where moments before she'd felt laughter and life.

The only solution she'd ever known for loneliness was work. She crossed the room to the desk and reached for the telephone.

"Say, you in the storage room, the one whose head is stuck in the refrigerator! Are you still counting, or what?"

Meghan pivoted to give a sheepish smile through the doorway to Tina, who sat at the waiting-room desk, tapping a ballpoint pen on top of it.

"I'm counting," Meghan said.

She'd gone to the storage refrigerator to see how many bottles of oxytocin were on hand so she would know how many to order.

It was bad enough that she'd spent a restless night dreaming about her encounters with MacDougal without what had happened to her a moment ago. When she'd opened the refrigerator and the interior light flashed on, she'd had another flash—the image of a Norseman with pagan eyes. For some off-the-wall reason she was reminded of Tarzan's mating call—and a sane, intelligent female simply did not react to a man by jumping up and down, yelling, "Me, Jane!"

This daydreaming about MacDougal had to stop.

"Who's Betty Bateman?" she asked Tina. Good grief, she thought. I'm cracking up.

"Widow. Two kids. Lives south of town. Nice lady. How many bottles of oxytocin are in there in that refrigerator, for crying out loud?" Tina questioned, her pen poised.

"Twenty-one," Meghan answered, closing the refrigerator. She went back into the reception room, crossed the room to the window and glanced out on Main Street, which was absent of traffic. No Shank. No Blythe— No! she chided herself. She would not allow her thoughts to slip back to Thane MacDougal.

Tina interrupted her thoughts. "I don't like to imply your heart isn't in taking this inventory and making out this order, but five minutes to count twenty-one bottles of oxytocin?"

"Preoccupied, I guess," Meghan replied.

"Why, I'd never have guessed that vacant stare in your eyes meant you were preoccupied," Tina teased her. "Now that I have your attention, how many dozen do you want to order?''

"Six dozen."

"Six dozen bottles of oxytocin coming up," Tina said, writing quickly. Without looking up from the supply order form, she asked, "Preoccupied with Betty Bateman?"

Meghan sat in a straight-backed chair in front of the window. "Her name came up when Murphy was here yesterday. Thane and Murphy are having supper at Betty's tonight. I just hadn't heard the name before, so I wondered who she was."

"The eyes have *it*, don't you think?" Tina asked. Having finished the order, she leaned back in the chair.

"Betty Bateman's eyes?"

"Sure, kiddo," Tina crooned, while her eyes accused Meghan of massive mental collapse. "Of course. Betty Bateman's eyes."

"So, all right," Meghan said. "Score one for yourself. Thane MacDougal has fascinating eyes."

A gleam danced through Tina's gray-green eyes. Meghan arched a brow. Was she reading Tina right? First Murphy had tried his hand at matchmaking, and now Tina was going to have a go at it?

Chapter Three

Bill and Thane and I have been friends since diaperhood. He's like a brother," Tina said, methodically folding the order sheet and slipping it into an envelope. "I figured you'd run into him sooner or later," she added, returning the envelope to the desk and sealing it.

Meghan slid sideways on the chair and hooked her arm over the back. "Run into him exactly describes it," she said, then quickly told Tina about the "nudge" at the grocer's freezer and her and Thane's second meeting in the bank door.

Tina smiled. "I knew you'd be interested in Thane once you met him."

"For heaven's sake, Tina, upon what evidence do you base that conclusion?" Meghan asked.

Tina shrugged, shoved the chair from the desk, walked to the cash register and punched a key. The register opened with a ding. Over the top of the register, she pinned Meghan with a knowing gaze.

"You want evidence? Well, for starters there's the sparkle in your eyes now and the flush on your cheeks. Then there's the question 'Who is Betty Bateman?' quickly followed by your denial that it was Thane's eyes we were talking about." Tina dipped into the register drawer and came out with bills and checks. When Meghan opted for silence, Tina prodded her, "Aren't you going to make a rebuttal so that I can argue convincingly on Thane's behalf?"

Meghan swallowed her laughter. "What's there to say? Your logic eludes me." She stood, walked to the freestanding shelves and began straightening the livestock markers.

"That tactic of insinuating that I'm being illogical confirms it," Tina said, sounding smug. "You're darn curious about Thane."

Meghan chose to talk to the wall rather than turning to face Tina. At least the wall wasn't ready to jump to erroneous conclusions...because the fact was, while she had been curious about Thane, she was no longer curious, so Tina was wrong. "Sorry, Tina. I'm not curious. Thane made one thing clear. Because I'm a vet, he wants to keep his distance from me."

"That's what the man says, but it isn't what he means," Tina said.

When Meghan glanced around, Tina was at her desk, counting the cash she'd taken from the register. "Thane sounded as if he meant what he said. I gather his marriage to a lawyer didn't work out."

Tina finished counting before she looked up. "Thane's never confided in me and Bill what went wrong in the marriage. But one thing was obvious when we visited them in Dallas. Cassandra demonstrated little fondness for Murphy, and a whale of a lot less for Thane."

"Perhaps Cassandra simply isn't an openly affectionate type," Meghan offered.

"Ah, but she is fond of one thing. She loves being a law-yer." Tina leaned back in her chair, thoughtfully tapping her finger on the desk. "She's an ambitious lady, driven to be successful. I'd guess she had little time for anything outside her professional interests."

The twist the conversation had taken struck a sensitive nerve with Meghan. There were times when she'd won-dered if she was too selfish about what she was doing with her life to share herself with a man. There had been men whose company she'd enjoyed—until it became obvious they were getting serious. Was telling herself she hadn't met the right man an excuse for avoiding the commitment of marriage?

"Trouble is," Tina was saying, "now Thane's got this stupid idea that what's right for him is a woman like Betty Bateman. Someone who doesn't threaten him with her in-dependence. But Betty would drive him crazy, because she's too much a clinging vine. Am I making myself clear?"

"*You* know what kind of woman is right for Thane. *He* doesn't," Meghan said a bit sarcastically.

"Take that smirk off your face, Meghan. That is exactly what I meant," Tina said. She took the bank's cash pouch out of her desk drawer, stuffed it with the money and zipped it closed. "Should I stick this in the safe until Monday, or do you want to take it with you?"

"Put it in the safe. I'll deposit it first thing Monday morning," Meghan said.

"Sure thing—unless you happen to get sidetracked in the doorway again and forget what you're doing," Tina said, chuckling.

"Highly unlikely," Meghan countered.

"Oh, I don't know about that. My intuition tells me you could be the right woman for Thane. And of course it fol-lows he could be the right man for you."

"I've always been a strong believer in intuition myself, Tina, until now," Meghan said, walking to the pet-supply section, which was located on another set of free-standing shelves.

"Sticks and stones," Tina said in a singsong voice. "The man has talents you wouldn't believe."

Meghan pivoted to give Tina a look that said, "You'll tell me about him no matter what I say."

"Thane's a fantastic cook," Tina said. "You should taste his sauerkraut and trimmings." To demonstrate just how good it was, she brought her fingers to her lips, kissed them and brushed the air.

The image made Meghan smile. MacDougal in the kitchen, with an apron tied around his waist? "You aren't listening to me, Tina. Nothing you can say will convince me that your intuition is right." She ambled to a wall display that held cattle supplies.

"You have a lot in common with Thane," Tina insisted.

Meghan glanced over her shoulder. "Really, Tina, why are you giving me the hard sell on MacDougal?"

"He's a nice guy. Romantic." Tina pulled out a desk drawer, fished around a bit and came up with a roll of stamps. She tore one free, licked it and slapped it on the order envelope.

Meghan looked at Tina, incredulous. Thane Mac-Dougal, romantic? A man who decided whether he was interested in a woman on the basis of whether or not she had a career? She looked at her watch and remembered that she had a ten o'clock appointment.

She walked toward the hall door, giving Tina a long, penetrating glance as she passed the desk. "Thane is romantic? Pardon my slang, but baloney!"

"No baloney. He—"

"Don't tell me anything more. I don't think I can handle it."

"He hooks rugs," Tina said, feigning penitence. Then she smiled impishly. "Sorry, Meghan. I couldn't help myself. I had to spit it out."

"Hooking rugs *is* something I've always wished I could do. But I'm still not impressed." Meghan was at the door. "Just because a man hooks rugs doesn't mean he has a romantic disposition."

"Of course not. But Thane does. He's just a slow starter."

Meghan wheeled in the doorway. "Oh, he got off to a fast start, Tina." She recalled his brushing pinch under chin, the sensation of spiraling warmth she'd felt with his touch, but she didn't want to confess that to Tina. Instead, she added, "But if he had any romantic feeling about me, he controlled it."

"So with you he got off fast on the wrong foot. For heaven's sake, Meghan, you can't expect him to display his romantic side until he trusts you." Tina paused, then added, "He's sexy."

"You aren't getting through to me," Meghan insisted. She didn't need Tina to tell her Thane was sexy. But it didn't make the problem easier to deal with. "If you're done with the sales pitch, Tina, I'm on my way to check a cow with mastitis. I'll be back in an hour."

"Boy, are you closed-minded," Tina muttered.

Meghan groaned. "Tina, have I ever gotten in the last word with you?"

"Not once!" Tina laughed, then just as quickly sobered. "There's more to this man than what you're seeing. Maybe you should—er . . ."

Meghan clasped her hands in front of her, tilting her head inquiringly. "Are you trying to find the words to suggest that I chase Thane MacDougal?"

"Dear woman!" Tina exclaimed as if appalled. "Chasing is so undignified. So immature. What we are talking here is being open-minded about Thane—until he gets to know you."

"But he doesn't want to get to know *me*, Tina," Meghan countered, then turned from the door. "If you need me, you can reach me on the radio."

She walked briskly down the hall, pausing at the kennel door to grab her coat. From the reception room Tina yelled, "I could have you both over to supper some night."

Meghan didn't answer. Why should *she* be open-minded? He was the one with the hang-up about women with careers. Thane MacDougal wasn't her problem, her project. Let someone else deal with him.

She left the clinic by the back door and slammed it behind her, meaning that to be her last word on the subject of Thane MacDougal.

Late the following Monday afternoon Meghan was standing at the window again, waving at Murphy as Thane backed Blythe from the curb. Murphy had been delightful company. His face had been rapt with concentration as he'd scrupulously swept wood chips from the kennels while she'd washed the cages with disinfectant.

There had been no pause in their conversation. Murphy had asked about her mother and father, their ranch in Kansas. She told him about her brother, Shea, and sister, Sue; about Mingo, her horse, and her twenty-five cows, all of which were at her parents' ranch.

Meghan had learned from Murphy that there was a drainage problem around the barns on the MacDougal place but that a bulldozer was coming in in the fall to correct it. Murphy's face glowed as he told her about Butternut, the heifer he'd raised on a bottle after Butternut's mother had rejected her. Murphy informed Meghan that his dad had once considered being a veterinarian but instead had decided to be a chemist. She also had discovered that Thane had been a vice-president in his grandfather's feed company before they'd come back to Iowa.

She and Murphy had been pigging out on potato chips and milk when Thane arrived. He'd been neither friendly nor unfriendly. It appeared to Meghan that, if anything, in the time Thane'd had to think about it, he'd grown stronger in the conviction that she wasn't eligible for "coffee." Absent today was the cordiality he'd exhibited when they'd met in the doorway of the bank and then again when he'd given her that warming smile. The compassionate side of his personality, revealed through Murphy's conversation, his sense of humor, the hint of passion she'd seen in his eyes when he'd touched her under the chin—he would keep a tight rein on those facets of his nature whenever he was around her, she knew. He was determined to keep their friendship at one notch short of friendly.

An absolutely horrible thought angled into prominence in Meghan's mind as she recalled the expression on Thane's face when he'd walked through the door and caught Murphy and her laughing over the fact that they'd consumed a large bag of potato chips. Did Thane think she might use Murphy to get to him?

The idea was repugnant. If he'd even consider that she'd stoop so low to get his attention, then he had a heck of a bloated ego. He might be attractive, but he certainly wasn't *that* attractive. Well, maybe he was, she corrected herself. But really!

She turned from the window. She'd had her last thought about MacDougal—forever. Let Betty Bateman worry about what the man was thinking, she decided haughtily. She'd had enough of trying to figure him out. But even as she was giving herself the pep talk she was wondering whether he'd call her if he needed a vet.

* * *

Three days, fourteen hours and some odd minutes later, Meghan was on the MacDougal farmstead, still telling herself she'd had her last thought about Thane MacDougal. During that time span, if Tina had even looked as if she might raise the subject of Thane, Meghan had squelched her. So Meghan had no one but herself to blame for the renegade manner in which her mind had behaved.

She sighed. She had no willpower when it came to Thane MacDougal. Time and again she told herself that there was no more fruitless endeavor than thinking about Thane. Time and again images of Thane popped into her mind and stayed like cockleburs stuck in a dog's hair.

Twenty minutes earlier Thane had called the office. It hadn't been to invite her out, as in her more or less insane moments she'd envisioned he would. He'd called because Butternut, Murphy's heifer, was in need of her services.

To her relief she discovered that hearing his voice hadn't shaken her in the slightest—at least not after she'd heard the politeness in his tone as he told her about the problem with the heifer. And she'd responded with businesslike formality.

While she drove to the MacDougal place through a heavy rain, she convinced herself that unlike what she'd thought, she hadn't physically responded to Thane. Those pricking sensations along her spine when he'd touched her under her chin and the warm way she'd felt when he smiled at her could be explained plainly and simply. She'd romanticized about the man, allowed her imagination to work overtime, even though he was hopelessly pragmatic, despite what Tina said. And romanticizing over any man was totally uncharacteristic of Meghan.

But today would put an end to it. They would come face to face, only this time he'd look like any other farmer, wearing a work shirt and blue jeans. The bothersome fantasizing would end and she'd deal with him with professional detachment.

She looked down at the muddy muck of the barnyard. Her last step had landed her six inches deep. Murphy had understated the situation when he'd mentioned the drainage problem around the barn.

Gingerly she lifted her right leg, leaned left and kicked the mud and manure from her overshoe. The clods plopped into the surface water of the barnyard, splashing watery muck on her yellow rain pants.

Of all the possible scenarios that had flashed through Meghan's mind about what would happen when she saw Thane again! She recalled the one where she waltzed to the door wearing a pale lime chiffon she'd been saving for a special occasion.

But here she was, waddling through a muddy barnyard, outfitted in rain attire: yellow hurricane hat, coat and suspender pants. Land, how the yellow clashed with the color of her hair, she marveled. But when she'd bought the outfit she hadn't been thinking about how appealing she would look, only how practical the gear would be.

No foresight, she concluded. But if he dared to laugh at her, if he even smiled, she'd throw her bucket at his head.

She tried to think of something positive about her situation. The only thing she could come up with was that the rain had lessened to a drizzle. She adjusted her equipment: in her left hand the obstetrical chain for pulling the calf, and in her right hand the steel bucket, which held soap, K-Y jelly, iodine and rubber gloves.

From under the rim of the hurricane hat she peeked out to see her destination. She knew Thane would be in the smaller birthing shed behind the barn. "Go through the gate by the barn and you'll see the building I'm talking about," he'd told her. And there was the shed, not twenty feet away, though it seemed more like a mile.

Before she'd entered the empty cattle yard, she'd called to him. He hadn't answered, but she was sure she'd heard a hammer being pounded and his rich tenor singing "Blue Eyes Crying in the Rain." He undoubtedly had her blue eyes in mind as he sang, she thought with a chuckle. What a joke. The thinking that was going on was one-sided—her side.

In an exaggerated step she threw forward her right foot, which she'd been dangling in midair. In an effort to balance herself she rotated her burdened arms as if she were a butt-heavy bird trying to take flight. When she tried to pull her left foot from the mud to bring it up to her right, nothing happened.

"I'm in trouble," she muttered. She was stuck, and like quicksand the mud was sucking her feet deeper, though she remained motionless.

"MacDougal?" she called. "Thane? Where are you?" In the distance, thunder answered. Lightning arced through the sky and disappeared beyond the wooded hill ahead of her.

There seemed to be no bottom to the mud. She was being pulled under. Good grief! A foot deep. "Mac*Dougal*! Where are you?"

"Well, hello," Thane said.

Meghan sighed in relief. Thane had opened the door of the birthing shed and was framed in the light of a bulb glowing from somewhere inside. He held a hammer.

Dampness had caused the tufts over his forehead to twist into tight, thick curls. He wore snug blue jeans that rode low on his hips. A green plaid shirt was tugged tightly over a broad expanse of chest. Dagnabbit, Meghan fretted, he *was* as impressive as she'd remembered.

And she looked . . . gross, she thought. She gave Thane what she feared came off as a Daffy Duck smile. "I think I need some help getting through the mud. I seem to be stuck."

Meghan looked down at her feet and demonstrated by trying to lift one and then the other. When nothing happened, she looked back at Thane. "See?"

"The evidence is indisputable. You're stuck. But frankly, Meghan, I'm getting as much pleasure from watching you squirm as you got from watching me squirm when I was trying to be diplomatic about Murphy's invitation to supper."

He knew he was just stalling. Meghan had been on his mind constantly, working herself into his thoughts when he least expected it. Her face would form in the newsprint of the newspaper he was reading. He'd heard the sound of her voice in the whisper of the wind through the branches of the oak outside his bedroom window, heard her laugh coming from a song being played on the radio.

And now he was seeing her, and he should be laughing. She was dressed in awful yellow rain gear, stuck almost to the tops of her overshoes, looking as silly as he felt. Except she didn't look silly. No matter how he regarded her, she looked marvelous. He put down the hammer, stepped into the barnyard and began plowing his way toward her through the mud.

"Frankly," Meghan said, "to me you sounded more dictatorial than diplomatic."

"Me. Dictatorial?" Thane asked.

"Yes. 'Maybe some other time,'" Meghan said, mimicking him.

Thane stopped in his tracks, hands on his hips. He couldn't resist teasing her. "Now I wonder whether I need to hear a pretty-please before I rescue your lovely hide."

"You're being childish!" Had he called her lovely?

"I know. Terrible of me, isn't it?" Thane grinned.

Meghan gnashed her teeth. She'd show him! She'd just pull every darn muscle in her body and get unstuck on her own. She grappled with the equipment and gave it a college

try—accomplishing nothing but a lot of undignified grunt-
ing.

When she reluctantly looked back at Thane, he was still
grinning. She glared at him. She narrowed her eyes to slits,
trying for furious.

Thane's grin broadened accordingly. "Now who's demonstrating a streak of childishness?"

"Cockroaches," she muttered. "All right. Please!"

"No need to be huffy."

"Huffy! Why in the world would you think I was being
huffy? I'm only stuck to my knees in your muddy barnyard
and you want to play games!"

"I love the way your eyes slant when you're having a
tantrum."

"I'm *not* having a tantrum. I'm having—fun!" Darn
him, she thought. Since he wasn't interested in her in any
way but professionally, why was he needling her in a voice
that crooned? Now, instead of feeling awkward, she felt utterly feminine, in an utterly unlikely circumstance. "But I
am tired of being stuck."

"I know you are, and I shouldn't have made you wait this
long before helping you," he said, moving toward her.

Meghan wanted to blister his self-confidence with some
scathingly witty retort, but as he advanced he fixed his gaze
on her, negating conversation. The combination of his smile
and those golden eyes was deadly. She was wildly happy to
see him. When he was close enough to see the joy she was
feeling, she said, in order to hide that fact from him,
"Murphy says you're getting a bulldozer in here this fall to
do some drainage work."

"Now that's an idea. I could leave you stuck where you
are and let the bulldozer driver dig you out."

Thane's delivery was monotone. There was no hint of a
smile on his lips. Only his eyes betrayed his humor. I like

him, Meghan thought. No, what she'd meant to think was that she liked a man with a sense of humor.

Thane was eye to eye with Meghan again, and he knew he'd blown nothing out of proportion when he'd fantasized about her. There was fire in her hair and in her eyes, and his body was kindled by the sensuous vibrations he felt coming from her.

"How do you feel about mud wrestling?" he asked. Brilliant, MacDougal, the cool, calculating side of him remarked acidly. He only hoped his remark was silly enough to keep her from guessing just how happy he was to see her again—happy despite the fact he knew how wrong they were for each other.

"I'm game if you are," Meghan said. She knew he was teasing and her heart was doing flips. There was no denying it; her response to him *was* on a sensual level. And no denying that she liked what she felt.

He extended his hand to her, and she believed that if he touched her she would burst into flame. Only some ingrained sense of propriety made her offer him her pail, instead of her body.

Thane was telling himself not to do anything impulsive, so he'd have nothing to regret, but he bent, cradled Meghan's legs behind her knees with his right arm, captured her upper torso in the curve of his left. As she draped her arm over his shoulder, he swept her from the mud.

What little had been left of sane thought fractured in Meghan's mind when she realized how close his lips were to hers. Her throat was parched as she said, "What are you going to do?"

"What do you want me to do?"

She ran the tip of her tongue over her lips. "Keep an open mind about me," she whispered.

Chapter Four

Keep an open mind," Thane repeated, mesmerized by the pink tip of her tongue as she moistened her lips. Whether she knew it or not, she was asking to be kissed. So he kissed her.

If Meghan had been feeling trepidation, the confusion left her the moment Thane's lips caressed hers and the softness of his beard brushed her cheek. The kiss was tender, whispering promises. Without reservation, she gave herself.

The moment Thane's lips touched the velvet silkiness of Meghan's lips, it dawned on him that he'd never experienced the real intimacy of a kiss. He knew he was feeling more than infatuation for her and should have broken the kiss off then, when it was no threat to his emotional independence. But he wasn't thinking, only feeling, and when her lips parted invitingly, he slid the tip of his tongue into warm recesses of her mouth and tested the sweetness. And in that succulence the barnyard was forgotten, the gently falling mist only an accompaniment to his pleasure. He was mindless of everything but the tingling sensation on his tongue as he probed the delicate flesh of her mouth.

When she curled the tip of her tongue lazily over his, every nerve in his body screamed for continuation, but with the scream for continuation came the realization that he tottered on a precarious ledge.

Reluctantly he ended the kiss, gazed for a moment at her lashes, then pinned his gaze on the shed and moved toward it, laboring under her weight and the weight of self-condemnation. Warm and responsive as she was, there could never be anything meaningful between them.

"I shouldn't have kissed you, Meghan," he said. "I'm sorry."

Meghan opened her eyes to discover Thane's jaw set in a determined line. "Sorry?"

"It was a mistake. One kiss could lead to another—"

"You sound as if you think I'm to blame for what happened. I was the kissee, not the kisser." Her face flamed. How *did* they get into these embarrassing exchanges?

"I don't think there's such a thing as a kissee. Anyway, you are to blame. You're kissable." He was breathing hard.

"Put me down. I'm too heavy," Meghan said. She was kissable?

"It's those boots."

"The boots?"

"They're loaded with mud," Thane said. "Heavy."

Meghan smiled, thinking, I'm kissable. She craned her neck to peer at her boots, which were indeed covered with mud. She shifted in his arms to distribute her weight. The obstetrical chain hit his thigh. "Sorry about that," she said.

"That's okay," Thane said, huffing.

Meghan used her arm that was slung over his shoulder to hoist herself up. The bucket banged against his back. "Sorry."

"'Sokay," Thane grunted. His breathing was ragged.

"Put me down," Meghan urged him.

"Never tackled a job I couldn't finish," Thane insisted while he considered throwing her toward the shed door. It was only a step away. She'd most likely land on her feet.

"Thane! You're going to drop me!" Meghan yelled when she felt his arms lowering.

"After my bravado of picking you up, there's no way I would drop you. I'd herniate first."

She laughed as he gathered himself for one last, lumbering step, took it, and set her on her feet just inside the door. He bent forward so she could ease her arm and the bucket over his head.

Meghan was thinking, how refreshing to meet a man who had enough self-confidence in himself to admit he had limitations. She brought her arm forward, and the bucket sounded a dull thud on the back of his head.

"Thane! I'm sorry. Are you all right?" Meghan asked.

He rubbed the back of his head, wincing. "Did you do that on purpose?"

"Why would I?"

"To get back at me for telling you I shouldn't have kissed you."

Meghan set her equipment down and turned toward Butternut. Thank goodness she had the excuse of taking a quick inventory of the situation. Thane had stanchioned the heifer in one of the stalls, and Butternut had been lying down but stood when they entered.

"I might *think* about banging you in the head with a bucket, but I'd never do it. Relax—I understand how you feel about me."

Thane found himself in the unenviable position of talking to Meghan's back. "I don't think you do."

"But I do," Meghan insisted. She glanced over her shoulder, a serene smile hiding her disillusionment. With the kiss she'd been prepared to allow whatever might happen to happen, but she could tell his mind was set against her in spite of his obvious desire for her. "I'm the kind of woman you want to make love to, but not the kind of woman you'd marry. How long has Butternut been in labor?"

Man! Thane thought. Talk about detachment. One minute she was kissing him until his toes curled, and the next she wanted to know how long a heifer had been in labor. Was that clinical or was that clinical! Damned right it was, and it just reinforced what he'd suspected: her professional life came first and her personal life second.

"About a half hour," he said. "The calf is in the anterior position. One foreleg is retained. And by the way, not that it matters, but that was a damned cold analysis of my kissing you—saying you're the kind of woman I'd want to make love to but not marry."

"Um . . ." Meghan said as she walked over to Butternut. "My mistake. I am the kind of woman you want to marry."

"I didn't say that," Thane said, exasperated.

Meghan gave him a sharp look, then turned to place a firm hand on the heifer's back flank. "Of course you didn't, Thane. You're right about the calf. It's in the anterior position. The sole of one hoof is showing down."

She stepped away from Butternut and took off her raincoat. She didn't have time now for a steaming rebuttal about his attitude toward her. She'd save that for when she was on her way out the door—and out of Thane MacDougal's life.

"Murphy says that at one time you thought about being a vet," she said, tossing her raincoat over a partition.

Thane evaluated Meghan's demeanor. Was she being contemptuous? "That was my dad's dream for me. I took three years of medicine and ended up as a chemistry major. I worked for a time in a quality-control program with a feed company. But my dream was to come back to the home place and farm."

"I always wanted to be a veterinarian. It's nice to know dreams do come true," she said, trying a smile out on his look of vigilance.

Thane had been prepared for an exchange of sharp words: fault-finding ones from her, defensive from him. Now he was hunting for something to say that would fit the occasion and take his mind off the way the artificial yellow light of the bulb was firing the russet of her hair, how the shadows were dancing across her cheeks like ghost lovers at play.

"So you were born to be a vet," he said. What in the hell was there about her that left him either running off at the mouth or inarticulate?

Meghan studied Thane's expression. Was he still being wary? Or was this where he started picking her apart for choosing a career in an area many perceived as a man's world? Meghan wondered. "I read recently that over half the veterinarian students today are women, so I wasn't alone in my dream," she said carefully. Not wanting to argue with him, she directed the conversation back to the calf. "Unless there's a problem I'm not seeing, Thane, I think you could have delivered the calf."

"I'll have to admit I thought about it, but when we saw Butternut was showing signs of parturition this morning, I promised Murphy I'd call you if she had trouble. I didn't want to chance anything going wrong."

Meghan nodded sympathetically.

"Dammit," Thane growled. "The truth is I wanted to see you again to prove to myself I was giving you more thinking time than you deserved. I'd hoped that after I saw you I'd be able to dismiss you."

Surely he was testing her sense of humor, Meghan thought. "Well," Meghan said. "Well." She wouldn't say what was on the tip of her tongue, that he'd been in her mind, too. "Uh, where can I get some water?"

"Faucet's in the corner." He'd managed to render her speechless with his impetuous outburst, he mused as she moved away. Had he expected her to say, "Well, in all honesty, Thane, I've been thinking about you, too?" She would be too busy to think about any man, let alone him.

And still he couldn't discipline himself. Right now he was looking at her and seeing how nicely her blue shirt fitted, calculating whether his fingers could span the circumference of her waist beneath the sloppy suspendered pants.

Meghan was sure it was the heat of Thane's gaze on her back that caused the prickling sensation along her spine. She glanced over her shoulder to confirm it. "Here's a little advice, MacDougal. That look you're giving me would better serve you if you gave it to someone you'd invite for coffee."

She hadn't intended the statement to be humorous. She was challenging him to make up his mind about her. Yet as if on cue, their laughter vibrated together off the walls of the shed, freeing Meghan to concentrate on the business at hand.

There was no conversation as she filled the pail, set the obstetrical chain in place and pulled on the rubber gloves. Butternut arched her back and hunkered as Meghan, murmuring soothing words, worked the calf into birthing position.

As he watched Meghan, Thane asked himself, What did I expect? That instead of being capable, she would be inept? She was far from that; she handled the heifer firmly, yet with movements that were both gentle and dexterous.

Once the calf was in position, Meghan attached the obstetrical chain above the calf's fetlock joints. When the heifer strained, Meghan applied a steady pressure outward and downward on the chain. A minute later Thane assisted her in lowering the calf to the straw bedding. Meghan dropped to her knees beside the calf, clearing its nostrils.

"Breathing's shallow and spasmodic," she said. She picked up a stem of straw and inserted it into the calf's nostril, hoping the tickle would make the calf sneeze. She massaged the calf's chest.

For a moment Thane watched the calf's sluggish effort to breathe, then he walked to the hydrant, where he washed his hands. Drying his hands on his jeans, he returned to stand over Meghan.

"I'm going to have trouble living with myself if the calf dies," Thane said. "I should have pulled him myself, instead of waiting for you."

"If it'll help ease your guilt, I wanted to see you again, too," Meghan admitted. "I'm sure he's just a slow starter."

As if to confirm Meghan's opinion, the calf's nostrils twitched. He sneezed, and every muscle in his sturdy little body twitched to life. Meghan sighed in relief. "Looks as if it's time for Butternut to take over, if you'll..."

Thane was on his haunches, next to her. With tantalizing slowness he extended his hand until his fingers caressed the back of her neck, urging her toward him. She could either go gracefully with the urging of his hand or resist and put them both in a pile.

When their faces were inches apart, Thane said, "That day in the bank doorway, the tip of your nose talked to me."

"And what did it say?" Her heart was pounding like a hammer on her ribs, and she wondered if she, too, was going to have difficulty breathing.

"It said, 'Touch me. I'll laugh.'" Thane touched the tip of her nose with an index finger.

Meghan's laugh came from delight.

Thane's laugh was spawned from hers.

Perhaps it happened because her laugh sang in Thane's ears so sweetly. Perhaps it happened because the encouragement he saw in the brightness of her eyes gave him some kind of confidence, or maybe it was the feeling of her heartbeat under his fingertips. Maybe it was inevitable, like the downward rush of a stream from a hillside spring, the swell of a bud before the flower blooms. He kissed her and in the kiss expressed a desire he'd never felt for any woman, then he pulled back and looked to see his feeling of shock reflected in her startled eyes.

He drew his fingers from the white column of her neck, then, because he was sure he couldn't keep from touching her again, he made a fist. "I do seem to have a weakness when it comes to touching you, don't I?"

Meghan understood that Thane wanted to skitter behind a curtain of humor again and that she could challenge his actions if she chose. But she was feeling too much too quickly and needed a respite so she could sort through her emotions.

She smiled. "Do you consider kissing me a temporary weakness, too?"

"That little kiss? That came from Butternut. She thanks you for Murphy. Taking care of Butternut helped Murphy through some rough times."

Meghan nodded. Rough times for Murphy meant adjusting to his parents' divorce, not seeing his mother as often as he'd like, feeling unloved by her. "So Butternut thanks me, does she? But do you always kiss the vet as a part of the payment?"

"This is a first," Thane said solemnly.

Meghan's eyes twinkled. "Thank heavens!"

"But you're the first female vet I've had on the place."

She groaned. "You say such nice things to me, Mac-Dougal. Thank you."

"You're welcome, Forester," Thane said lightly. Then his voiced deepened with emotion. "Meghan, I do appreciate the fact that you don't back me into a corner and demand I explain myself when it comes to you."

"No explanation needed. I'm kissable."

Thane grinned. "You are that."

She washed her gloves, then stripped them off. How could she demand an explanation of him when her own behavior was inexplicable?

She collected her equipment while Thane released Butternut from the stanchion. When the heifer backed up, sniffed out her calf and began cleaning its creamy red hair with short strokes of her tongue, the calf made its first attempt at a serious bellow.

"Oh, man!" Murphy's exclamation came from the open shed door. "Hi, Doc. What did Butternut have, and is she okay?"

"Hi yourself," Meghan replied. "A bull. And she's fine. If she hasn't cleaned in forty-eight hours, call me. How did school go?"

"Okay," Murphy said as he wandered to Butternut, patted her neck, looked the calf over and smiled like an indulgent father. "I'm going to sing a duet with Charlene Kant during the spring concert at school. It's on the fifteenth of May. I know it's a month and a half away, but do you want to come, Doc?"

"Only the sky falling would keep me away. I'll write the date on my calendar."

Listening to the easy exchange of conversation between Meghan and Murphy, Thane thought about the times Cassandra had promised to put Murphy on her calendar, then broken the promises. Now Meghan was promising to put Murphy on her calendar. Thane was sure her intentions were good, but did she understand that what would seem like a small promise to her would mean much more to Murphy?

Meghan saw the troubled expression on Thane's face. She sighed in spite of herself. Just when things seemed to be going right between them, something went wrong. She knew she'd done nothing to upset him. At the same time she had no doubt somehow she was responsible for his frown. She reached for the bucket.

"You want the bucket emptied?" Murphy asked.

"Please," Meghan said.

Murphy took it from Meghan's hand, carried it to the door and gave the water a heave. "Did you make doughnuts today, Dad?" he asked as he wandered back and stood waiting for Meghan to put on her raincoat.

Meghan smiled at Thane. "Tina said you're a fantastic cook. But doughnuts?"

With a part of his mind Thane found it enticing to know that Meghan and Tina had been discussing him. Yet she could be thinking, How quaint, or how eccentric, a man in the kitchen making doughnuts.

"A man can make doughnuts if he wants to, can't he?" he said, taking neutral ground until he could establish what she was thinking.

"You'll get no disagreement from me. My dad is the steak, salad and cinnamon-roll person at home," Meghan said.

Thane gave her a foolish grin—as foolish as he felt—then compounded his foolishness by saying, "Some of the best cooks in the world are men."

"That's a fact," Meghan said. She glanced around the shed to make sure she didn't leave anything behind.

"And some of the best veterinarians in the world are women," Murphy added. "Doc, you have to stay for lunch."

"Maybe Meghan has another call," Thane suggested.

Meghan ignored the cryptic overtone of Thane's statement and smiled. "I do have one more call, but I think I have time for a doughnut. It's been a long time since I ate homemade doughnuts. Glazed? Cake?"

"Cake. Buttermilk," Thane replied.

"Great! What are we waiting for?" Meghan asked.

Thane fastened the shed door, and Murphy and Meghan plodded through the barnyard toward the gate, Murphy carrying the pail, and Meghan the obstetrical chain.

"Pretty easy to get stuck in this mud," Murphy remarked.

Meghan chuckled, but then the memory of the kiss she and Thane had shared streaked through her mind like a shooting star. Regardless of what he'd said, the barriers between them had momentarily tumbled. And tumbled again with their second kiss, she was thinking when he joined them. He took the chain from her hand.

She smiled in thanks, only to be greeted by the same dour look he'd given her when Murphy had invited her for lunch. Such a sour face wasn't called for, she thought, a bit miffed. He wasn't obligated to a whole life with her, just the time it took to eat one darn doughnut.

Any lack of enthusiasm on Thane's part, however, was compensated for by Murphy's lively conversation as they left the barnyard and crossed the lane to Meghan's pickup.

"Doc's mom and dad have a cattle ranch in Kansas, Dad," Murphy said. "She helps brand cows, and she's got twenty-five head of 'em. She even has her own horse. What do you think of that?"

"I'm impressed." Thane gave him the eye. If Murphy said anything about Betty being afraid of horses...!

"Not everyone knows a real cowgirl, Dad," Murphy said as they reached Meghan's pickup.

"Not everyone wants to know a real cowgirl," Meghan retorted. She'd caught the warning look Thane had given Murphy.

Why, he was acting like a pouting brat, she thought. And if anyone was justified in pouting, she was. He tantalized her one moment by arousing her expectations and disappointed her the next by treating her like a pesky fly. She slipped from her rain attire and placed it in one of the back equipment compartments.

"Nice pickup you got, Doc. Flashy red color," Murphy commented.

Standing first on one foot and then the other, Meghan pulled her overshoes off and slipped her cowboy boots into lightweight galoshes. "I'll have to admit the color sold me. Where's Blythe?" she asked as they started across the lane. The only vehicle in sight was a small car.

"Blythe's in town getting a paint job," Murphy replied. "Grandpa always said when he got Blythe running again he'd paint her blue, the color she was when he and Grandma bought her in forty-eight."

"Blythe's been on the road since forty-eight?" Meghan questioned, looking at Thane before she remembered he was being a grump. He was still being a grump, but he answered.

"Blythe spent about eight years stored in the garage, waiting for a new transmission and body work," Thane said.

So Shank hadn't been stretching the truth when he'd compared Thane's treatment of Blythe with his treatment of women, Meghan thought. Thane was refurbishing the pickup, not neglecting it. Did it follow that he didn't neglect Betty?

They moved across the lawn of browned bluegrass toward a two-story frame house. Pale yellow with brown trim, the house had a full front porch, which gave it a welcoming look. It was toward the back of the house, though, that Murphy led them.

Murphy pointed to a dinner bell mounted on a pole. "We plant salvia and petunias around the pole," he said, then directed Meghan's attention to a narrow band of turned earth running along the sidewalk. "And we put our four-o'clocks here. The blossoms draw a lot of hummingbirds, and having the four-o'clocks here makes it easier to watch the birds.''

"Maybe Meghan isn't interested in the design of our horticulture, Murphy," Thane said.

Meghan frowned at Thane, smiled at Murphy. "I am interested. Do you get any hummingbird moths, Murphy?"

"We sure do, but I didn't know they were moths till Dad showed me the difference." He led the way across a brick patio and up the steps of another full porch.

Meghan grudgingly admitted that while Thane was one heck of a poor host, she continued to be impressed with him as a father—and she really did sincerely hope Betty Bateman liked playing in the dirt, she thought, almost smirking.

On the porch, they removed their overshoes and set them on a bristle mat.

Thane, finished first, moved to the door. He was still chewing on that "Not everyone wants to know a real cowgirl" line Meghan had tossed him. If Murphy weren't all ears, Thane would have answered her challenge by asking what would be his advantage in getting to know a cowgirl.

"Would you like coffee to go with the doughnuts, Meghan?" Thane asked as he held the door open for her. He'd be courteous but maintain his distance, that's what he'd do.

Coffee? Meghan thought. She'd need it to warm her. Thane's tone of voice was like a winter wind, she thought as she stepped through the door and into a large mudroom that also held a washer and dryer.

When Meghan glanced over her shoulder, Thane was looking at the ceiling. The message was clear: *You're here but I don't have to like it*. Be polite, she told herself. No shin-kicking.

"Please," she said. "That is, if you were going to make some coffee for yourself, I'd have a cup."

"I was," Thane said.

Meghan removed her denim jacket, and Thane reached to take it. While she was firm in her conviction that it would be a cold day before she'd ever again consider Thane in a romantic light, she made sure her fingers didn't come in contact with his when she passed him the jacket.

"Thank you," she said. She couldn't wait to dunk her doughnut and be gone.

"You're welcome," Thane said. He hung her jacket on a wall hook next to his work jacket. And there they were, he thought, two denim jackets hanging side by side, looking for all the world as if they were meant to hang side by side.

"Where do we wash up?" Meghan asked. When Thane looked at her as if she'd made a suggestive remark, she stammered, "I—I'd like to wash up."

"Oh, sure! You want to wash up. Murphy, show Meghan to the upstairs bathroom. I'll use the one down here and then get the coffee started."

A moment later they were standing in the kitchen, and what began as a glance around the room for Meghan turned into a slow, appreciative appraisal. While every modern convenience from appliances to culinary tools was in evidence, to step into the kitchen was to step into the past, where the illusion was that the pace of life was slow and easy.

The four-burner countertop stove was mounted in a center-counter chopping block. Above the stove, suspended from a grayed wooden-spoked wheel, was a variety of pots and kitchen utensils, some brass, some cast-iron, some wood. The oak cupboards glowed from being hand-rubbed with oil. A lush ivy hung in a window over the sink.

"This is a beautiful room, Thane. Rustic and peaceful," she said at last.

"Thank you," Thane said, sounding calm, feeling desperate. For his sake, for Murphy's, he had to maintain distance between himself and Meghan. But how could he play Mr. Cool when her smile was inviting a thaw?

Chapter Five

Murphy grabbed Meghan's hand. "Come on. I'll show you the front room on our way upstairs."

The long and wide front room turned out to be no less rustic and homey than the kitchen. A rough rock fireplace dominated one end of the room. An old but newly reupholstered rose sofa, two leaf-green easy chairs and some oversized end tables with stacks of books and magazines were the primary furnishings of the room.

Meghan moved to a huge hooked rug centered on the floor. A black border set off the flower-leaf pattern of rose, yellow, cream, green and brown. "Tina said your dad hooks rugs. Did he do this one?" she asked Murphy.

"It took him one whole winter. Do you hook rugs?"

"No," Meghan said, "but I'd like to try someday when I have the time. Which way to the stairs?"

"Bet Dad would teach you to hook if you'd ask him," Murphy said. "Come on. The stairs are this way." He led her down a long, wide hall, then turned left. "And after we

wash up I'd like to show you something else. Something
Dad made."

"You wouldn't be trying to get your father and me together, would you, Murphy?"

Ahead of her on the steps, Murphy looked over his
shoulder, all innocence.

"You might as well give up on the idea, because it isn't
going to work."

"That's what Dad said. He said Betty was more his
speed."

Murphy appeared unabashed while Meghan discovered to
her chagrin that her nose had been shoved out of joint.
Betty was more Thane's speed! Then what was she, Meghan
Forester? Too fast or too slow? Either way, Meghan didn't
like it.

They were quick in washing, Murphy setting a world record and in the process leaving some of the dirt he'd had on
his hands as smudges on the towel. Once again in the hall,
Murphy swung into action, tugging Meghan away from the
stairs.

"Come on, Doc. You've got to see Dad's bed."

"Murphy, I don't think your dad would like that."

"Betty's seen Dad's bed," Murphy said cunningly.

Without further discussion, Meghan followed the de-
signing little devil down the hall. A smile flitted across her
lips, then faded. She wasn't jealous—or anything remotely
resembling it—but under what circumstances had Betty seen
the bed?

Murphy guided Meghan into Thane's bedroom. "There
it is, Doc," he said, indicating the king-size, four-poster bed
that dominated the room.

"Hello again, Finnigin," Meghan said, walking to the
bed. She bent and ran her fingers over the kitten, who was
curled up, sleeping. Finnigin unfurled, stretched.

Murphy was standing at the end of the bed. When Meghan looked at him, he put his hand on the post. "Dad turned the posts from a walnut tree Grandpa had cut down," he said, still in his role as tour guide. "But he had to order the mattress and heater. It's a water bed."

"It's very nice," Meghan offered. She was impressed with Thane's handiwork, but she didn't want to encourage Murphy in his matchmaking project.

As she straightened from petting Finnigin, she glanced around the room. Two large oil paintings of country scenes hung on the wall over the bed. A massive dresser, a rocking chair—her gaze stopped at the antique chest of drawers. On it sat several pictures.

"That's my grandpa and me," Murphy informed her. "We were getting ready to go bullhead fishing on the Big Sioux." A very young Murphy and an elderly man were sitting on the front porch steps, cane poles in hand, a Pekingese stretched at their feet. "And the other picture is a picture of my grandma. She died when Dad was three."

The portrait was of a light-haired, lean-faced young woman who had been captured with a serene smile in her eyes. Thane had been motherless at three? And now he himself headed up a single-parent home. Her heart went out to him. She couldn't imagine having grown up without the nurturing support of her mother.

And yet even after two generations of male domination, the house showed no lack of a woman's touch. It certainly was not the stereotypical bachelor pad. In fact, stepping into the MacDougals' kitchen had evoked the same sense of tranquillity she felt whenever she stepped into her parents' kitchen.

"You have a water bed, Doc?" Murphy asked, bringing Meghan back to the moment.

"No."

"Ever slept on one?" He sidled close.

Meghan smiled. Ah, yes, there was scheming lurking in those green eyes of Murphy's. But she was confident she was ahead of him this time. "No, I've never slept on a water bed—and I'm not interested in getting onto a water bed, either, Murphy."

"Gosh, Doc. Dad won't care."

"I have my boots on. I'd get the comforter dirty." The comforter was quintessential country, a calico print of blue, brown and cream.

Murphy puckered his lips. "It's too bad you won't go for a test ride. Betty did."

"Give me a second to take my boots off." Meghan went to the wicker rocker, sat and removed her boots while Murphy dropped to the floor and took off his tennis shoes. "Why are you taking off your sneakers?" she asked, having the good sense to be suspicious.

"I'm the one who makes the motion."

"The motion?"

"You know, Doc. The up and down." Murphy got up. "You have to have motion, Doc."

The up and down? Meghan stood, moved to the bed. A wise person would have exited when the gleam in Murphy's eyes developed into a look of barely controlled let's-get-on-with-this, she knew. Betty "the right kind of woman" Bateman had gone for a test ride, and Meghan could not let it be said that Meghan "the wrong kind of woman" Forester had failed to meet the challenge.

"All right," she said. "You provide the motion, but how do I get in?"

"Well, you back up, throw your arms out and fall back," Murphy advised.

"Back up, throw my arms out and fall back?" Meghan walked in reverse until she felt the bed board on her legs. Murphy was backing up, too. She looked down at him. "Are you sure this is the way you're supposed to do this?"

"You bet!" Murphy grabbed her hand. "Here we go!" he yelled, then threw himself backward, taking Meghan with him.

Meghan squealed. The mattress gave with a squishing sound. She felt a wood platform on her back, then rode a tide upward, laughing.

"Great, isn't it?" Murphy hollered.

Meghan turned her head to discover that while she'd been riding the wave, Murphy had managed to get into a sitting position with his legs crossed, hands on the mattress, pumping with his arms. His pumping resulted in another tide. Meghan squealed again. Murphy's laughter bounced off the wall, while Finnigin, an old pro, rode the wave as if she were on a surfboard, then stood braced on the pillow, tail up, riding out the gale.

Meghan laughed with Murphy but wondered if it was possible to get seasick in a water bed. After two more upheavals, she was sure it was possible. She threw her arms out and tried to still the motion of the water.

"It's free flotation. Good for your back," Murphy announced.

"That's nice, but now that I know how it works, you can stop pumping." Meghan was like an overturned turtle rolling side to side as she tried to get an elbow under herself so she could sit up.

Thane had followed the sound of shouts and laughter up the stairs. He wasn't surprised to discover Meghan on his bed, cavorting with Murphy. What he wasn't prepared for was the intense sensual excitement he felt at finding her on his bed—and the tug on his heart at seeing the uninhibited expression of joy on Murphy's face. "What do we have here?"

Meghan thought she could hear a chuckle in Thane's voice, but all she could see was the very top of his wheat-colored hair framed in the doorway.

"I, uh, went for a test ride," she said, thrusting her head forward. She caught a glimpse of his forehead before a wave took her beyond that perspective. He didn't appear to be frowning.

"This is Doc's first time in a water bed," Murphy said.

Thane walked to the bed and looked down on Meghan. Her face was flushed. He got images of lovemaking through the night, heated bodies, morning sun streaming into the bedroom window. "It's free flotation," he mumbled. "Good—"

"For your back. I know. Murphy told me," Meghan said. "But I seem to need some help getting up." She raised her arms. "Please."

Thane extended his hands to hers. Her hands in his felt small, her skin pliant against his callused palms. He drew her to her feet and for a moment could neither drop her hands nor look away. The sweet provocation of having her a hairbreadth away held him transfixed.

Meghan was entrapped in the web of a golden gossamer gaze where her mind and body were gently being seduced to conjugate with his. So when he dropped her hands and turned from her to walk to the door, she followed him, mindless.

"Hey, Doc," Murphy called, "don't forget your boots."

She'd forgotten them, forgotten Murphy, forgotten there was a world outside. In that rarefied air she and Thane were breathing, he obliterated her sense of self, of time, of place.

She turned to Murphy, smiling. "Guess for a moment I was still dizzy from all the motion," she joked.

A few minutes later they were downstairs at the table and Meghan was mumbling around the doughnut in her mouth, "This is delicious, Thane."

"Dad makes great pizza, too, Doc," Murphy said. "Bet he'd make some for supper if you'd stay."

Thane shook his head. Murphy had first launched his "Dad, why don't you take Doc out" campaign on the way home from the clinic the day Finnigin had her distemper shot. But now Murphy had gone too far, Thane decided. Meghan was blushing.

"Murphy," he said firmly but not unpleasantly. "Meghan and I can be friends without you pushing us."

He and Meghan hadn't discussed the possibility of being friends. He hadn't even thought about it until it popped out of his mouth. He waited to get Meghan's attention and then, with his eyes, asked for confirmation that friendship was the status they were working on.

She nodded. The telephone rang. Thane excused himself and rose to answer it.

He moved sensuously, Meghan mused. With masculine dignity, she amended as her gaze traveled from his legs to his tapered waist to the expanse of his shoulders. His green plaid shirt only hinted at the muscles she'd felt when he'd carried her to the barn.

"MacDougal residence," Thane said. "Oh, hello.... Nothing much. Did Mary Jane get over her cold?"

"That's Betty Bateman," Murphy said. "Mary Jane is four. She goes to preschool with Nance Greer. Chip says their teacher, Mrs. Blair, told Mr. and Mrs. Greer that Mary Jane and Nance gave her an ulcer."

Meghan swung her gaze back to Murphy, expecting to find him joking, but there wasn't a trace of a twinkle in his eyes. "Mrs. Blair has to be teasing, Murphy. Nance is a darling."

"Nance is pretty cute, but once in a while she's something besides darling," Murphy said, shaking his head as if pondering Nance's dastardly deeds.

Thane was saying, "The vet's here." Meghan came alert. And when he said, "Delivered Butternut of a bull calf," the hair on the back of her neck stiffened. The *vet*? He could

have called her Doc or Miss Forester. He'd carried her obstetrical chain, hadn't he? Wasn't that the same as carrying
her books to the bus after school? The vet indeed!

Murphy leaned closer and confided, "Betty told me that
she doesn't know the difference between a cow and a heifer.
Can you *believe* that?"

Meghan found herself now in the position of defending
the woman. "I don't know much about hooking rugs, and
I'll bet Betty does."

"I don't know if she does or doesn't, because I never
asked her." Murphy rested his elbow on the table and
propped his chin in his hand. "Betty's okay. But she isn't a
guy...like you are, Doc. You think it's fun to do what guys
do."

Meghan's lips twitched in merriment.

Thane overheard Murphy's comment. He glanced at the
table and saw Murphy gazing intently at Meghan. Her eyes
were bright. Thane gnawed his lip to keep from laughing.
He'd do a little more explaining about the birds and bees
and see if Murphy still thought Meghan was a *guy*.

"Uh, what, Betty?" he asked. "Oh. We're having coffee
and doughnuts."

"Bet Betty asked why you're still here," Murphy observed.

Thane was suddenly impatient, but he realized the impa-
tience wasn't directed at Murphy, as it should have been, but
at Betty. He wanted to be sitting across the table from
Meghan, watching her eyes animate her expressions, listening for the inflections she used in speaking. Couldn't Betty
take the hint that he was busy? He'd told her Meghan was
here and they were having coffee.

"What?" Thane ran his fingers through his hair while
Betty asked him again if he would like to go with her to do
some shopping in Sioux City. He said, "Afraid I can't make
it, Betty. I've got sows coming in."

"Bet Betty asked Dad to do something with her that he doesn't want to do. She's sweet on him and asks him to do a lot of dumb things with her," Murphy said.

Meghan just blinked. She wouldn't allow herself to comment on that one, even mentally.

"Excuse me a minute, Betty." Thane cupped his hand over the mouthpiece. A couple of dates and a couple of suppers at Betty's and she was trying to monopolize his time, he was thinking. But Murphy was pushing the limit of his patience by telling Meghan that Betty wanted him to do a lot of dumb things with her, even if her idea of "fun things" bored him to tears.

He turned to his son. "Murphy! That will be enough of the running commentary. You hear?" Without waiting for an answer, he went back to trying to listen to Betty.

Murphy slid down in the chair as if he acknowledged the reprimand, but he winked at Meghan, then rolled his eyes.

"Murphy," Meghan whispered firmly, "your father is talking with a friend. How would you like it if you were talking to Chip and I was making smart, belittling remarks about him?"

Murphy looked as if she'd slapped him. She wanted to rub the frown from his brow and speak soothing words, but he couldn't be allowed to make fun of Betty, no matter if the woman wasn't a "guy." "You know I like you, Murphy. But the way you're acting is wrong, and your father is justified in being angry with you."

Murphy nodded and sank back against the chair, shoulders slumped.

Thane said goodbye and replaced the receiver. In a moment he was looming over the table. "Murphy, I don't like to reprimand you in front of company," he said, stern. "But if you can't say something nice about Betty, don't say anything."

"I'm sorry Dad. Doc already told me I was behaving bad. She said you were right to be mad and how would I like it if she made smart remarks about Chip. Do you want me to call Betty and apologize?"

"No. Betty didn't hear you. The matter is dropped."

Meghan stood. "Guess it's time for me to roll. Thank you for the doughnut, Thane, and the tour, Murphy."

"You have to go already, Doc?" Murphy said. "I thought maybe we could have a game of Monopoly."

"I'd love to stay, Murphy, but I really don't have time. Remember? I told you I had another call. I'm due at the Miller place by five. But how about having supper with me some night? We can play Monopoly then."

Murphy shoved his chair back and stood. "I can come this Saturday night," he announced decisively.

Meghan picked up her cup and saucer and went to the sink with them. "If Saturday night is all right with your father, it's certainly all right with me."

"Gosh, Dad. Doc invited you, too."

Meghan was in the process of setting the dishes in the sink and nearly dropped them. The little fox! "I didn't exactly mean I was inviting your father," she stammered.

"You don't want Dad to come? We could have a great game of Monopoly with three of us."

"I . . . well, your father is probably busy." She looked to Thane for help. "You're busy, aren't you?"

"Not that I know of," Thane said, sounding guileless. It was his turn to sit back and enjoy the action. Now she was getting a taste of how it felt to be cornered by Murphy.

"Dad's not busy," Murphy told her.

"I heard," Meghan said.

Thane flashed a smile. "What's on the menu, Meghan?"

Boiled water, dammit, she thought. Can the innocent act, she told him silently. "What would you suggest?" To herself she asked, Why, oh why, would you, who failed home economics, ask a gourmet what he wanted on the menu?

"I really have no preference," Thane said.

Meghan heaved a sigh of relief. She'd play it safe and go with a roast. Maybe toss in a potato or two—

"How about sauerkraut and trimmings?" Murphy suggested.

Meghan paled. Murphy sounded as if *everyone* knew about sauerkraut and trimmings; *she'd* never heard of the dish until Tina mentioned it. She edged toward the door, pausing before opening it."

"Actually," she said, then saw Thane was very interested in her answer. Too interested. "It's been a while, but I'll give sauerkraut and trimmings a shot." Good grief, she was taking up stupidity as a cause.

"Sure wouldn't want to miss sauerkraut and trimmings," Thane said. It was all in the cause of establishing their friendship, he told himself.

"Then we'll plan on having supper...say, sevenish," Meghan said airily. She opened the kitchen door and stepped into the mudroom. Thane and Murphy shadowed her movement.

"Supper at sevenish sounds utterly delightful," Thane said, mimicking her airy attitude. He'd lay odds the lady had never heard of sauerkraut and trimmings. "But will that give you enough time to prepare supper? You do keep the clinic open until three on Saturdays, don't you?"

Just the way Thane was mimicking her attitude and the way he'd tilted his golden head and stroked his beard as if meditating told Meghan that he was on to her, that he knew she didn't know a stinking thing about making sauerkraut and trimmings. Enough time to prepare supper? What did *that* mean?

Meghan took her jacket from the hook. "I'll be on a tight schedule, but I'll manage. Thanks again for the coffee and doughnut."

"Sure," Thane said.

At the same time, Murphy said, "Boy. I can hardly wait until Saturday night, Doc."

"Neither can I, Murphy." She wished she had half the confidence in herself that Murphy was expressing.

"I've got homework to do, Doc. Thanks for coming out. And come back to visit anytime." Murphy vanished into the kitchen with Meghan's goodbye following his retreat.

"I think he decided we needed to be alone," Thane said.

"Don't be too hard on him for trying to arrange something between us. He'll give up in time."

"Oh, I expect he will," Thane said. He leaned against the doorjamb, one leg crossed over the other just below the knee, his arms folded. Casual he wasn't being, he knew. He needed bracing, for Meghan's effect on him was physically draining.

He needn't have sounded quite so happy about Murphy's giving up, Meghan reflected as she waited for Thane to say something else—anything to fill the silence. But all he did was lean against the doorjamb, looking at her with what appeared to be an air of arrogant boredom. Well, she certainly wouldn't waste any more of his time. She lifted her jacket to slip her arm into place.

"Allow me." Thane stepped to take the jacket from her.

"Certainly," Meghan said. She turned her back to him and slipped her arm into place. Her body was singing a sweet melody and urging her mind to sing along, but she told herself she was firm in her determination that the body was going solo. That resolve might have lasted, but then Thane leaned closer. Soft puffs of warm air from his steady breathing caressed her ear, and it was to that warmth her body yielded.

"Murphy's wonderful," she said in a rush.

Thane's body was invaded by her presence; his blood was warmed by her, and then the warmth surged in waves with his heartbeat and he had to force himself to check his impulse to draw her length to his.

"Thank you for telling Murphy that he could have hurt Betty's feelings. I think you made a bigger impression on him than I did," he said.

His beard brushed Meghan's ear. An avalanche rumbled in her head. The earth pulsed violently beneath her feet. From the chaos came a roaring question: Why wasn't he concerned about her feelings? Did he assume that because she was a veterinarian she lacked the sensitivity of other women?

When her right arm was in place and she felt the weight of her jacket on her shoulders, she stepped away, wheeling to face him. "Is Betty sweet on you?" she asked.

"Would you be jealous if she were?"

"Why would I be jealous? I know where I stand with you. Friends, you told Murphy. And I assume Betty is in the eligible-to-have-coffee-with category."

"She is in the right-woman category. But she's not the right woman for me," Thane said almost sadly. "I've known it for some time. We don't have much in common. At least not enough to justify continuing to see each other."

"I don't believe you! Just like that, no more Betty. You could consult her, you know. She might have an opinion about the subject." When she realized what she was saying Meghan said, "Wait a minute! I don't know why I'm defending the woman. I don't care how coldhearted you are toward her."

"I'm not coldhearted. I'm concerned about how Betty feels," Thane countered, heating from the flare of anger he saw in Meghan's eyes. "Betty's made it plain that she isn't in love with me but likes the idea of having a man around to head up the household again." He stepped toward Meghan, though he'd intended to back away. "She's looking for someone to make her decisions for her. Now, I don't know about you, but I happen to think that's a darn poor reason for anyone to get married."

The hot winds of emotional upheaval left Meghan's sails. She was contrite, barely capable of looking Thane in the eye. "I apologize. Actually, it's too bad you couldn't get together."

"Is it too bad?" Thane closed the gap between them. She'd been closing her jacket snaps, and he took her hands. Meghan looked down. She'd ended two snaps out of line. He undid the jacket and resnapped it. "Is this going to work?" he asked, thinking about whether or not they could be friends.

"It will now that the snaps are lined up," Meghan said, purposely ignoring his meaning. She couldn't help herself. She was glad Betty was out of the picture.

"I'm not talking about the jacket. I'm asking if we can be friends and keep our relationship on an impersonal level," Thane said.

Impersonal level? When he touched her she trembled. Was that impersonal? "I don't know," she said, gloomy.

"I don't know either," Thane admitted, feeling sullen. "But it might work if we had some ground rules about the chemistry we have going here. I'm not dreaming it up, am I, Meghan? Something does happen when we touch."

Meghan couldn't flinch, couldn't hide from the questioning probe of his gaze. "Something happens," she acknowledged.

"Can we even be friends?"

Meghan moved to the door, opened it and stepped outside without answering. She leaned against the side of the house while she slipped on her galoshes.

From behind her, still in the doorway, Thane said, "Murphy likes you, Meghan. He trusts you. He needs your friendship."

"I know."

"Doesn't it follow that if we allowed this attraction we have for each other to develop beyond friendship, after whatever we feel ran its course the strain between us would put a strain on your friendship with Murphy?"

Land, he had a way with words, she marveled. *Attraction beyond friendship* was a euphemism for *affair*. So she'd been right all along about one thing. She was the kind of woman he wanted to make love to, and grudgingly she admitted she admired his honesty. Physical attraction was what he felt, and when it was over it was over, take it or leave it. Well, she wasn't taking, no matter how tempted she was.

"You're right," she replied. "If we got involved in something personal that ended unpleasantly, it would put a strain on my friendship with Murphy. But just to set the record straight, Thane," she said sharply, "I don't make a habit of getting personal on a casual basis."

Thane answered her sharpness with some of his own. "I didn't think you did."

"Thank you," Meghan said bitingly.

Thane stifled a laugh. He'd given Meghan the opportunity to say that whatever they had going might mature into something more enduring than infatuation, that she might grow to care enough about him to make time in her life for him. And she'd scoffingly rebuffed him.

"All right. You won't consider dating a man like me," he said cryptically.

Meghan reacted vehemently. "Why do you twist around everything I say? You're the one who can't visualize yourself with a woman like me. At least not out of bed."

In a flush of adrenaline, Thane's heart hammered and his face grew warm. "What I can't visualize is you taking time to play a game of Monopoly with Murphy!"

In that instant Meghan hated Thane MacDougal with a passion she'd never felt for another human being. Never had anyone made her feel so vulnerable, caused her such heartbreak, with so few words. Without thought he'd trampled on the very core of her femininity, by insinuating that she wouldn't make a good mother.

Shaking and close to tears, she swung away, leaving the porch. "You're right," she said hoarsely as she cleared the last step. "If we're going to be friends, we'll have to have ground rules."

For the first time in her life Meghan was running from a confrontation. But she couldn't handle herself at this point. She would either deteriorate to a state of blubbering or try to wring his neck. Neither option seemed viable. But by the next time she saw Thane MacDougal, she told herself, she'd be prepared for him. He wouldn't get another opportunity to hurt her.

Thane wheeled into the house and, in an expression of abject disgust with himself, slammed the door behind him. He'd seen the tears glistening in Meghan's eyes before she'd turned away. He balled his right hand into a fist, pounded it into the left.

What the hell was all that insane talk about being friends, anyway? Friendship between them was unachievable. And Meghan knew it as well as he did.

Chapter Six

Meghan was in bed, propped on pillows. She dog-eared the page of the paperback she'd been pretending to read, placed it on the bedside table and picked up the card on which Tina had earlier written the recipe for sauerkraut and trimmings.

On the way into town that afternoon, Meghan had had a heated debate with herself. In a diatribe she'd convinced herself those things she'd found appealing about Thane MacDougal didn't exist. He was an uncaring brute. Had that man lived in the days of rubbing sticks to get sparks, he really would have clubbed a protesting female over the head before dragging her off to his cave. Tina just didn't know how romantic the man was!

By the time Meghan was halfway into town she'd decided to cancel the supper invitation. She didn't give a cockroach if she ever saw Thane MacDougal's intriguing face again. The next time he needed a vet, she'd tell him where to go.

Then she'd argued with herself that no matter how she felt about Thane, she had to be mature enough not to allow her feeling for him to influence her relationship with Murphy—because that is exactly what Thane expected to happen.

By the time she reached town she'd decided to salvage what little remained of her dignity and proceed normally with supper Saturday night.

Having made that decision, she'd stopped at the Greers' to see if Tina had the sauerkraut-and-trimmings recipe. As Tina handed Meghan the card, she'd said, "Cut the recipe by three-fourths or you'll have enough to feed a battalion."

Now Meghan tilted the card to the light of the bedside lamp. Fifteen ingredients were listed, among them bacon, spareribs, pork shoulder roast and Rhine wine. Juniper berries? The supper she'd committed herself to making took three hours to cook, not even allowing for preparation time. Providing there was no emergency on Saturday and she came right home from the clinic at three o'clock, she would have to be riding some lucky streak in order to have the meal ready by seven.

Groaning, she glanced at the clock. Eleven-thirty. Was she going to spend the next five nights sleepless over crushed juniper berries and chopped onions? For heaven's sake, she chided herself, it was only a meal.

She tossed the recipe card back onto the bedside stand, shut off the light, reclined on the pillows and closed her eyes. The worst possible thing that could happen would be Thane pronouncing the meal inedible—which wasn't beyond the realm of possibility, considering how beastly he could be.

And what were the possibilities of their having a friendship? What kind of friendship could it be when the relationship made her feel as if she were lost in a maze?

And then there was this capricious side of herself that she'd discovered, which surfaced when she was around him. She'd always believed she knew herself, and she'd always been predictable. But *he* triggered unpredictability.

Was there a chance something more than physical attraction could be causing her emotional turmoil? Could she be—no! How could she be falling in love with a man who couldn't accept her vocation? With a man who was so insensitive as to imply that she wouldn't be a good mother?

She couldn't be, and that's all there was to it, she was thinking when the telephone rang.

Anticipating an emergency call, Meghan slid her feet from beneath the covers to the floor and switched the light on before picking up the receiver.

"Dr. Forester speaking."

"Hello, Meghan."

Though there was no sound of urgency in Thane's voice, Meghan's heart started beating double time. "Hello, Thane. Something go wrong with the calf or Butternut?"

"No. Everything is fine. Catch you busy?"

Meghan returned to her propped position on the pillows and tugged the blanket over her feet. "I'm almost always busy at midnight," she said, a little sarcastically.

"Stupid question."

"Stupid answer." Her reflection in the dresser mirror showed she'd turned pink from the neckline of her white nightgown to her hair. She'd felt herself grow warm a few times when Thane had looked at her, but had she blushed like *this*? If she had, it was no wonder he'd deduced she felt something.

"You were sleeping," he stated.

"Actually, I was reading." She slowly ran her toes over the sheets, curled them.

"Me, too. A farm journal."

"Historical novel on this end. In fact, I just put it down." She hadn't really lied.

"Uh, I just remembered I didn't pay you for this afternoon," he said.

She might have known he was calling for a practical reason, Meghan thought. "I'll have Tina send you a bill."

"I'm lying. I didn't call about that," Thane said. "I was trying to read, but I couldn't."

There was a long pause in which Meghan heard his soft intake of breath. She could see his cat eyes, smell the freshness that seemed to be a part of him. She wondered what detergent he used to wash his clothes. Did he wear shorts or pajamas to bed? Was his chest light-skinned or faded tan from last summer's sun? Her mind's image had her body responding with tremulous tingling, when his voice shocked her back to the moment.

"I called to apologize for that crack about you having no time for Murphy, for bringing tears to your eyes."

So his conscience wouldn't allow him to sleep. Maybe he wasn't so terrible as she'd been thinking. Still, she wasn't quite prepared to expose her soul to him so his could be soothed.

"You don't have to apologize. I don't cry often, but I've been known to cry at inappropriate moments," she said. "One time I blubbered up a storm because a neighbor's dog dug up my petunia bed."

There was a gentle laugh from Thane, followed by an even gentler tone of voice. "I have the feeling you make every effort to shed your tears in private. I don't think you're comfortable exposing any vulnerability—but then, neither am I."

It was *that*, Meghan realized, Thane's intuitive knowledge about the workings of her inner thoughts, that made her unpredictable when she was with him. His intuition also made her defensive. He *knew* her. And he could hurt her.

She was vulnerable with him when she'd never been vulnerable with another man. That was how he was different from any man she'd ever known.

"Meghan," he was saying. "You're sweet and sensitive, and I was being insensitive today. I didn't mean to hurt you—I'd never intend to hurt you. And I wanted you to understand that."

"I know you didn't mean to hurt me, Thane," Meghan said. Then she confessed, "What upset me was the implication that while you think I'm capable of being Murphy's friend, you didn't think I was capable of being a good mother." She twisted the telephone cord in her fingers.

"I wasn't insinuating you wouldn't be a good mother, Meghan. Honest to God I wasn't. You'd be a great mother. I just believe if I ever marry again Murphy would benefit from having a full-time mother."

"I didn't know mothers punched a time clock," Meghan said frostily. The man couldn't put three civil thoughts together without being—good grief! He was confronting his feelings honestly. What did she want him to do, lie?

"I've done it again, Meghan, haven't I? Hurt your feelings. I'm sorry again, but I won't defend myself."

"Oh, Thane, I'm the one who should be apologizing. You're being honest in telling me how you feel, and I'm being critical of you. You're Murphy's father. You know what's best for him."

"Listen," Thane said abruptly. "I'll understand if you tell me to fix my own supper Saturday night while you entertain Murphy. Friendship between us could be too complicated."

"What are your ground rules for the friendship thing?" Meghan asked. "Or haven't you had time to think about it?"

"I've had time to think about it," he said.

Meghan heard the laugh in his voice. She smiled, stretched languorously in the bed, nestled her head in the pillow. "Are the rules hard to follow?"

"The difficulty level fluctuates. Number one, no sharing the same sofa."

Without having to face Thane, meet his gaze, having to deal only with the sound of his voice, Meghan could handle the sensuous lassitude of body and mind. "Easy," she said. "No sofa sharing.

"No brushing of hands," Thane said. "And a distance between us of three feet at all times should help to defuse the chemistry."

"I'm beginning to get the picture." Her voice was low. "No looking kissable from me, no incinerating looks from you."

"Do I give incinerating looks?"

"I'd assumed this friendship was going to be based on honesty," she said.

"Do you mean the look you told me to save for the eligibles?"

"That's the one." Meghan closed her eyes, opened them. Either way she saw that "sun tea" look of his.

"It will take some work for me to keep my thoughts platonic," Thane admitted.

"Me, too. But I think the honesty of this conversation has gone a long way toward defusing the chemistry, don't you?"

He panted in her ear. She laughed.

"Good night, Meghan."

"Good night, Thane."

Thane sat staring at the phone. He'd called Meghan not only to apologize for hurting her feelings but to tell her it would be best if they limited their relationship to only those occasions when he would need her professional services.

What had happened then? All at once they'd been revealing truths about themselves through intimate banter.

He knew he liked Meghan because she was tender-hearted, sweet, caring and beautiful. And because of the physical attraction, the situation was complicated enough without his taking the risk of falling in love with her. For the sake of self-preservation, the sensible thing for him to do was back off now. He could call her: she'd still be awake. He could tell her that on Saturday Murphy would be coming alone.

He reached for the telephone, but it rang before he touched it. He picked up the receiver and brought it to his ear.

"I don't want to complicate your life, Thane," Meghan said. "Maybe it would be best if you didn't come with Murphy Saturday night. Okay? I could drive out and pick him up."

The woman was reading his mind from three miles away. "You've complicated my life already, Meghan. I didn't want to care about you, but I do." He stared out the kitchen window. Moonlight was filtering through the branches of the tree outside. On the windowpane, branch shadows embraced like lovers.

"I know you care about my feelings. That's obvious," Meghan was saying in soft, flowing tones.

"How could you know, Meghan?"

"Because you couldn't sleep until you apologized to me."

"Are you sure it's caring that I feel and not simple lust?" Thane asked slowly.

"It's caring. And—chemistry. But lust is too strong a word, Thane. Whatever the attraction is between us, it falls short of lust. Right? I mean, we are restraining ourselves. Almost. We're being logical. Almost." She laughed.

Thane knew her laugh was a good-natured attempt at poking fun at how they were acting. "Yeah, sure. We're *almost* restraining ourselves. So why, whenever I'm with you, do I feel as if I'm taking a free-fall without a parachute? The

truth is, Meghan, I don't know if I can control what I feel
for you physically. I don't know if we can be friends—or if
we should even try. Does that scare you?''

''Not much scares me, Thane... and I've recently discovered I have more of the daredevil in me than I'd believed. I think we can be friends, but you have to decide
about Saturday night. If you walk through the door with
Murphy, I'll slip into my parachute and take the plunge into
trying to be friends with you.''

Through his laughter Thane heard Meghan saying,
''Good night, Thane,'' and then he heard the dial tone.

''Good night, my sweet Meghan,'' Thane whispered.
Sweet Meghan? How could he control himself physically
when he couldn't even control his thoughts? She did scare
him. She scared him almost as much as he scared himself.
How many times would he have to get cut down before he
learned his lesson?

Thane pulled Blythe to a stop in front of Meghan's house,
allowing the wipers to clear the windshield of snow before
turning off the pickup.

He'd dropped Murphy at the Greers. A month ago Tina
had promised to take the kids to the circus when it came to
Sioux City. The circus had arrived three days ago. Late this
afternoon, she'd called to say that at the last minute she and
Bill had decided tonight was the night they were taking the
kids to the circus.

He'd asked Tina if the circus was a ruse to arrange for him
to be alone with Meghan. Tina had only laughed, neither
denying nor confirming it. But when Murphy had accepted
the change of plans without protest, Thane had known for
sure that the two had schemed together.

Thane slipped his gloves on, and drew up the collar of his
overcoat. A blizzard was brewing, and the snowfall had al-

ready started. With the weather threatening to get crazy, he doubted the Greers would go to Sioux City.

Talk about crazy. This was crazy—his coming alone to Meghan's for supper. There was no reason for him to be here, save one. He wanted to be with Meghan. He knew that should have made him unhappy with himself. It was yet another example of his lack of self-discipline when it came to her. But he wasn't unhappy. Rather, his spirits were soaring like a kite caught in a spring breeze.

"Make sense out of that, MacDougal," he mumbled. He picked up a sack that held a quart of elderberry-grape wine his dad had made.

A minute later he was standing on the front porch at the door, shaking the snow from his hair and stamping the snow from his overshoes. He took a deep breath and rang the doorbell.

When Meghan didn't answer, he peeked through a nearby window. There was a light on at the back of the house. Kitchen, probably. Maybe the bell wasn't working. He pounded on the door.

Nothing. She had to be inside; it was almost seven. But maybe she'd been called into the country and the snow had slowed her down in getting back. He left the porch and made his way through the snow around the house, heading for the garage. In the driveway were tire tracks, but they were drifting over. He couldn't tell whether the pickup had been going in or out.

Feeling like a sneak and praying Meghan's next-door neighbor, the widow Green, wasn't watching him, he looked through the garage window. In the darkness of the garage's interior he saw the darker shadow of Meghan's pickup. She *was* home. He frowned. Why in blue blazes didn't the woman answer the door?

As he turned from the garage he saw Mrs. Green waving from her kitchen window. Thane waved, grinned sheep-

ishly, then, head down, trudged back through the snow to
the front of the house. As he rang the doorbell, Mrs. Green
shoved aside her front-room curtain.

Thane acted as if he didn't see the elderly woman at the
window. He banged on the door. He listened for Meghan's
voice, watched for the front-room light to come on. Could
she have been overcome by fumes from a badly vented fur-
nace? The flu was going around. Could she be in bed and
too sick to answer the door? "Meghan?" he yelled.

Testing the door, he found it unlocked. His scalp tingled.
He eased the door open and, stepping inside, called
"Meghan?" No smell of gas fumes. He closed the door,
then squinted and waited for his eyes to adjust to the dim
lighting. "Meghan?"

He removed his overshoes, set them on a rug in the en-
try, then moved farther into the room. Everything appeared to be in order. Sofa, chair, stereo and television,
slippers by the sofa—thieves would have taken the stereo, at
least.

He was being infantile. Beaver Crossing was hardly the
crime capital of the world. And with the town snoop, Mrs.
Green, watching Meghan's house like a hawk, if there had
been unidentified intruders around, the law would have been
sitting outside when he drove up.

Still, there *had* been a rash of burglaries recently. Hell,
someone had even backed a truck into the alley behind Ed
Reemer's gas station, broken through the back door, loaded
six tool cases and trucked them away. And Reemer's was
across the street from the police station.

But he was still being unreasonable. Meghan was not
locked in a basement coal cellar while someone burglarized
the house. He laughed at himself. His laugh sounded like a
sonic boom in the quiet of the house. Deadly quiet.

"Meghan!" he called as he walked toward the light at the
back of the house. He discovered the kitchen. There was no

evidence that Meghan had started supper, no smell of spice
and cooking pork to indicate the meal was in the oven.

On the other hand, there was no evidence of a struggle
with an assailant, either. In fact, the kitchen was immacu-
late and looked seldom used.

"Stop it!" he muttered. When the refrigerator hummed
on, he jumped. The house creaked. What could have happened to her? He hadn't had his fill of looking into her eyes,
heard enough of her laughter. Their relationship—whatever it was—had barely begun. She just *had* to be somewhere. All he had to do was find her. His hand was shaking
as he set the wine on the table. His heart was racing, his
breathing shallow. Okay! If this wasn't panic he was feeling, it was a darn good imitation.

He left the kitchen, hurried down the hall toward another soft glow of light, rushed past the open bathroom
door and charged into the bedroom. He was standing at the
end of the bed when he realized he'd found her.

Her arm was slung over the edge of the mattress; her fingers dangled, limp. Her denim shirt was unbuttoned, rum-
pled. Her head on the pillow was turned sideways, her
kissable lips slightly slack; her eyes closed. The mounds of
her breasts rose and fell while she slept—she was sleeping!
He was out of his mind with worry and she was sleeping!

"Dammit, woman!" he yelled. "Where'd you leave your
brains?"

Meghan's rude awaking was accompanied by a wild slap-
ping of the mattress as she jerked to a sitting position.

"Supper isn't ready," she stammered, blinking herself
awake. "One of the Sandburns' sows had a..." What was
he doing in her bedroom? And he'd *yelled* at her.

"I know supper isn't ready." He regarded her sleepy eyes,
tiny russet ringlets of hair at the nape of her neck.... He
wanted to retreat from the rigid guidelines of behavior he'd

set for himself; he wanted to go to her, cuddle her, tell her how relieved he was to know she was safe.

Meghan watched the intimate journey of Thane's gaze over her face, down her neck. Goose pimples rose wherever his gaze traveled. When her nipples pebbled she realized her shirt was unbuttoned. Dazed, she thought, He doesn't even have to touch me to get a "chemical" reaction. She folded the shirt over her breasts. "What are you doing in my bedroom?" she demanded.

"I was looking for you. You didn't lock your doors before you lay down!"

"Would you please stop yelling at me?"

"I'm sorry. I didn't know I was yelling," Thane said, then, realizing he was still yelling, lowered his face. "But you deserve to be yelled at."

"What did I do? I'm sorry about supper, but sows have a poor sense of timing."

"The hell with supper." Thane unbuttoned his overcoat, took it off, then draped it over his arm. "Didn't you hear what I said? The door was open. Anyone could have walked in...found you like this.... Anything could have happened."

"Are you saying you yelled at me because you were worried about me?" Meghan asked. She shifted higher on the bed. His shirt was a lush brown, soft-looking.

"Yes," Thane admitted.

"Then since you were worried about me and not angry because supper isn't ready, I forgive you for yelling at me, Thane. Uh, the house has only one closet—this bedroom closet—so why don't you put your coat here on the bed?" she suggested, leaning forward to pat the end of the bed.

"I didn't offer you an apology, Meghan." Thane was mumbling, and he knew it. He dropped his gaze from her eyes to her lips. No better, he thought. He tossed the coat to the bed and backed to the doorway.

Meghan gnawed her lip. There were no bones in her body, only nerve endings that vibrated deliciously. She was without an ounce of shame. She loved the way Thane's eyes were blazing warmth into her body, and if he didn't stop looking at her as if she were a cherished possession, she'd blurt out, "Forget the friendship thing. Try kissing me."

"You should have apologized, Thane," she whispered. "But you don't need to worry about me anymore. I'm perfectly safe with you, aren't I?"

"Yes. You're perfectly safe with me," Thane said, but he was thinking she *wasn't* safe. If he stayed one second longer, the meager ration of sanity he had remaining would vanish. He'd start ripping off his clothes.

He spun in the doorway. "I'll start supper," he called as he made a hasty departure.

Meghan leaned back, weak. Where was Murphy, her parachute? With him as a witness she could feel safe that she wouldn't slip from the friendship mode—at least, she was pretty sure she wouldn't. But Thane looked so utterly, magnificently male. Now, why did he have to show up dressed in brown? Didn't he know rich brown made his golden hair appear even more golden; his almond eyes even more catlike? If he didn't want to tempt her, why did he do that?

Chapter Seven

The delicious smell of simmering spices and bacon bits drifted to Meghan's nostrils before she reached the kitchen door. She threw back her shoulders, welded a smile onto her lips for Murphy and waltzed into the kitchen.

Oh, my, she thought when she saw Thane at the stove with a huge dish towel folded in a triangle and tied around his waist. Her eyes had to be playing tricks with her mind. There was no way the man could look even *more* virile wearing a dish towel.

Thane glanced at her as she entered the kitchen. He then snatched up a clove of garlic, put it on the chopping block and hacked away. Now why did Meghan have to go and do that, come floating in on a puffy pale lime-green cloud, smelling heavenly? Her dress accented the neatness of her waist, the smooth curve of her hips, but dammit, her neckline was too low to be demure. Didn't she *know* this platonic friendship was never going to work unless she cooperated?

"Where's Murphy?" Meghan asked, her waltz brought to an unceremonious halt when she realized she'd have to free-fall today.

"I dropped him at the Greers. Tina and Bill are talking about going to the circus if the weather doesn't get worse. I tried to call earlier to tell you about the change of plans, but you didn't answer." Well, he *had* allowed her phone to ring twice, hadn't he?

Meghan's brain was mummified. His dark brown dress pants fit his hips and thighs—should she give in to the sensuous feelings fighting to control her, or should she try laughing at herself for seeing him in a romantic light? Either way, her response was the same: Wow—the man looked great!

"I, er, didn't answer because I wasn't home. As I told you, I was at the Sandburns'."

"I didn't know that when I called," Thane said. He blended the chopped garlic into the ingredients simmering in the frying pan.

"Why did you come alone?" Meghan edged her way to the table, putting it between herself and Thane, then placed her hands on the back of a chair.

Thane stirred. Hot damn. She'd asked the big one. I came, my sweet Meghan, because when I'm with you I feel young and optimistic and unreasonably happy. "I thought you'd probably already started supper," he replied, realizing too late that she'd see right through that—he'd just told her he'd called and she hadn't answered.

"That doesn't wash, Thane," Meghan said. "Please, try again."

"All right. I came to see how our friendship would stand the test of being alone."

"And what does that mean? That you've changed your mind and instead of being friends, lovemaking is on the menu?"

"I have not changed my mind," Thane said, trying to sound indignant. Downright *injured*, he hoped. He glanced over his shoulder, making his eyes wide, innocent. Very hurt. "How could you even suggest that possibility, Meghan? I came because I wanted to see how compatible we'd be—that kind of thing." He went back to stirring.

Meghan thought he didn't look *that* hurt. He could have at least admitted he was tempted to make love to her.

But maybe she felt the attraction more than he did. "Why don't you stop that infernal stirring and look at me?" she asked. When he didn't stop, she took the initiative and walked toward him. She would make him look at her if she had to wedge herself between him and the stove.

Thane felt her closing in on him; her perfume caused him to feel light-headed. He stopped stirring and half turned from the stove. "Stop where you are. That's three feet."

Meghan raised her arm to measure the distance. "It isn't three feet. It's four, at least."

"Whatever it is, it's close enough," Thane said. Oh, what her eyes did to him. Taunting and laughing. He went back to stirring. "Stop fooling around. Don't you want to be friends?" he asked gruffly.

"Of course I want to be friends! I wasn't fooling around. I only intended to help. What can I do?"

Thane added a measuring cup of crushed juniper berries to the pan. "Chop the onion," he said. "Do you always sleep without locking doors?"

Meghan got out the only apron she owned, a horrible faded peach-colored thing. She slipped it on and reached behind her to tie it in place.

"When I lay down, I'd only intended to rest. I had a long day," she said. "Starting with an emergency at four in the morning."

Thane chanced a glance at Meghan. His heart skipped a beat. As she tied the apron, the material of her dress was pulled tight, revealing her form. Warning bells pealed in his brain. He forced his gaze back to the frying pan and stirred with a crazed frenzy.

"Hmm, four o'clock makes an early start," he said.

Meghan moved to the counter. Thane had taken her pig-shaped chopping block from where she had it hanging on the wall and set it on the counter. She *never* used her pig for chopping. She thought of it as decorative, not functional. She opened a drawer and took out a knife and began peeling the onion.

"You look tired, Meghan. Shadows under your eyes," Thane said, smiling sympathetically.

Meghan's smile was menacing. "Thank you for the lovely compliment."

"Dammit, Meghan," Thane said. He put down the wooden spoon and pivoted toward her. "You floated in here on a green cloud, smelling sweet, looking beautiful, but I'm not going to tell you that lime green makes your eyes look bluer than blue—we agreed to keep this friendship platonic."

"Yes, Thane. We did agree to keep it platonic," Meghan said. Her gaze didn't waver from his. "So I won't tell you that cocoa-colored shirt brings out the predatory cat color of your eyes."

Thane felt a rumbling of sensual thunder rocking the room. "I'm certainly glad you didn't tell me that," he said, grinning. "I don't think I could have handled a compliment like that gracefully. But you do look tired. Why don't you go into the front room, sit down and rest and allow me to fix supper."

Meghan shook her head and went back to work on the onion. She had it peeled. She started slicing and immediately began blinking to hold back the tears. "I couldn't sit while you worked. You're supposed to be my guest."

Thane was ready to peel and core the apples, which presented a problem in strategic movement. The apples were on the counter near Meghan. If he tried to get them from where he was standing, he'd be reaching in front of and across her. And if his arm accidentally grazed the chiffon—he was miserable. Blissfully miserable. He walked around Meghan instead, feeling very noble for his gallant decision.

"Where do you keep your paring knife?" he asked as he picked up an apple.

The knives were in the drawer at Meghan's waist. She batted her eyes. "I'll get it." She stepped back and opened the drawer. She looked down and pulled out a knife and laid it on the counter.

"That's a boning knife," Thane said.

"Oh." To Meghan, anything smaller than a butcher knife served as a paring knife, but she supposed a gourmet wouldn't use a boning knife to peel an apple. She put the boning knife back in the drawer, pulled out a smaller knife and set it in front of him.

"That's a filleting knife."

"Use it," Meghan said, slamming the drawer shut with her hip. "The paring knife is dull."

"I could sharpen it. You do have a sharpener."

"No, I do not have a knife sharpener, but even if I did, my paring knife is beyond even your expert help. I used it for a screwdriver, broke the end off, and now the poor thing is residing in dull-blade heaven."

Thane laughed. Meghan cried. She blinked and used the back of her hand to wipe at the tears, but that only brought more tears.

"A little hint about chopping onions," Thane advised. "If you'd slice the onion in half, use the flat as a base and hold the onion together as you worked with it, you'd get fewer tears."

"Is there anything you don't know about cooking?" Meghan asked snidely. He'd given her the worst possible job to do, then criticized the way she was doing it.

"I doubt it," Thane said thoughtfully. "My mother died when I was quite young. I can't remember a time when I didn't cook. Guess my cooking came about because I had a flair for it and Dad liked doing dishes."

Meghan felt a new flush of hot tears surfacing with those already awash in her eyes. What an insensitive clod she was, to feel defensive and accuse him of one-upmanship.

"Thane, I'm sorry I sounded snide," she said. Her voice trailed away as she resolved not to be quite so quick-tempered.

"You asked a question. I answered," Thane said. Her hair shone with highlights he'd seen in the setting sun; the darker, huskier tones of red he'd seen in the leaves of sumac in the fall. "I'm ready for that onion," he added, determinedly abrupt.

Meghan set the knife aside and with both hands scooped up some pieces of onion, carried them to the stove and tossed them into the frying pan. Grease spattered. She started to repeat the process, then decided she'd save time by taking the whole chopping block to the stove. There was a bit more grease spatter. Meghan felt pleased. When she glanced at Thane, who was hovering at her shoulder, however, she found quite the opposite expression on his face.

"All right. What did I do wrong now?" she asked crossly, thinking her resolve to be even-tempered hadn't lasted long. But it was his fault. He was being overbearing and patronizing.

"You don't scoop and throw anything into hot grease. You could get burned."

"You are not talking to a child, Thane MacDougal. I didn't get burned," Meghan said. Her face felt flushed. Her body burned. He was too close. She stepped the required three feet away. It didn't help. "I'm starting to wonder about this friendship thing. You're awfully bossy."

"It's not working out worth a damn to this point, is it," Thane agreed. "It's hard to believe you're so careless here in the house when you're so meticulous with your work."

"Aha! I knew it! You do think all women belong in the kitchen!" she exclaimed.

Their gazes clashed before Thane went back to dicing the apples. "You're wrong," he said. "I said what I *meant*. I'm talking about your disregard for your personal safety— sleeping without locking the damn doors, carelessness with hot grease." He viciously diced the last apple into a small bowl.

"You're nitpicking. As I told you, I was in a hurry when I got home and forgot to lock the damn doors. By the way, that's the third bowl you've used," Meghan snapped.

"Who's nitpicking? Not me! But it's occurred to me that we do seem to be getting on each other's nerves. Maybe I should leave," he growled as he turned to face her.

"Absolutely not!" Meghan said. "No way are we giving up on this friendship thing. We're going to work on it until we get it right—for Murphy's sake. And," she added as a token peace offering, "it's okay if you used three bowls."

"If it's okay for me to use three bowls, you can take your hands off your hips and the glare out of your eyes," Thane said. In her anger her eyes smoldered; the slight puckering of her lips made them appear even more kissable. He smiled. She hadn't given up on him.

Meghan hadn't realized she'd taken a defiant stance. She dropped her hands. "What's next into the pot?"

"How often have you made sauerkraut and trimmings?"

"Never." Meghan set her pig in the sink. It would probably warp when she washed it, she thought, but for the moment that didn't matter; Thane was smiling at her. She turned toward the refrigerator. "I acted as if I had because I didn't want to look bad in front of Murphy. I'll get the sauerkraut."

"No matter what you did or didn't do, Meghan, you could never look bad to Murphy."

Meghan smiled gratefully at Thane over the top of the open refrigerator door. She took the sauerkraut from the refrigerator, shut the door and set the sauerkraut on the counter by the meat and the Dutch oven. "What do I do now?"

"Want to butterfly the chops?" Thane asked.

"Sure," Meghan said. He could be so darn sweet, she thought as she positioned herself for meat cutting. Without making an issue of it, he'd taken the correct knife from the drawer and placed it next to the chops. But how the heck did one butterfly? Maybe if she just started kind of cutting around, something would come to her.

She sneaked a glance at Thane to see if he'd noticed her indecision. He'd gone to the refrigerator. He got out a quart jar of purplish-red liquid she hadn't put inside or seen when she'd reached for the sauerkraut.

"What's that?" she asked. "A substitute for the Rhine wine?"

"No. We'll use the Rhine wine for the trimmings. This is a little drink my dad made out of elderberries and grapes," Thane said.

He shut the refrigerator door and carried the quart jar to the counter, opened the cupboard and took down two small glasses. "Thought I'd pour us each a glass for sipping while we finish preparing supper. I don't know about you, but I could stand some mellowing." He gave her a sheepish grin, poured her a small glass and set it on the counter close to her.

Meghan picked up the glass. "Your father made this? How old is it?"

"I'd guess ten years, maybe." Thane poured himself a drink. "Dad was never one for labeling. Only brewing."

Meghan had never been a drinker, but she felt she could stand a little mellowing, too. And if a ten-year-old brew would mellow her, she'd drink it, because it was painfully obvious that she wasn't going to make it through the evening alternately feeling faint when Thane looked at her and fuming when he tried to instruct her. She took a sip.

"Not bad," she announced, winking conspiratorially. Thane winked back in a playfully flirtatious way that instantly corrupted her good intentions of keeping their relationship platonic. With a flourish she set the glass down and started working on the chop again.

"Meghan! What *are* you doing to that chop?"

"I'm . . . deboning it." Meghan stared down at the hapless chunk of meat.

"Looks like overkill to me," Thane said, deadpan.

Meghan reached for her glass, sipped and eyed Thane over the rim. The drink was smooth, tart and sweet; it left her tongue tingling. This sip was noticeably warmer going down than the first had been. As she studied the features of Thane's face, she decided that while he could be sweet and endearing and fun, he was also decidedly argumentative.

"You'd better slow it down, Meghan. That stuff you're drinking like pop packs the wallop of a Moscow mule," he said. He exchanged eye thrusts with her. "Dad called it the Stinger."

For a moment Meghan continued to play eye games with him while trying to decide how honest he was being. Packs the wallop of a Moscow mule? Baloney. He was just being bossy again.

Giving him a defiant look, she drained the glass, then extended it to him for a refill. He muttered something but poured her another quarter glass.

"Oh, be a little more generous, Thane. These are small glasses," Meghan said flippantly.

"Have it your own way," Thane said, filling the four-ounce glass and handing it back to her.

"Thank you," Meghan said. "Now, isn't this getting to know each other for the sake of friendship fun? Where were we? Oh, yes. We were indirectly discussing my lack of expertise in the kitchen. So I don't know how to butterfly a chop. I do have my own forte: junk food."

"Your forte is being a veterinarian. You don't have time for a lot of cooking," Thane said, thinking that she shouldn't joke about her eating habits. She should take better care of herself. She shouldn't be living on junk food, not the way she expended energy.

Meghan chafed from his words: *Your forte is being a veterinarian.* She doubted that he was trying to be complimentary. She wasn't marriage material because she was a vet. She wasn't mother material because she was a vet. And now, dammit, she couldn't cook because she was a vet.

"My being a veterinarian has absolutely nothing to do with why I can't cook," she argued. "The simple truth is that even when I have time to cook I don't cook because I don't *like* to cook. Now, if that takes away from my femininity—"

"Nothing could take away from your femininity, Meghan."

Now this was sticky, Meghan decided. How could she keep herself under control emotionally when he lowered his voice and tossed out a line like that? Heavens. She felt an old-fashioned swoon coming on...

"Thank you for saying that, Thane. I liked it," she said. Her gaze dropped to the pork chop. She'd killed it, poor thing. She stifled a giggle.

"You're welcome," Thane said. He turned the stove off and carried the frying pan to the Dutch oven. "But you owe it to your health to learn to do more in the kitchen than heat frozen dinners. Good grief!'' he said, exasperated with himself. ''I'm trying to tell you how to take care of yourself.''

''I don't think you were doing that—exactly.'' She was feeling generous because the discussion wasn't about her cooking but about her health, which wasn't any of his business either, but she didn't have the heart to tell him so because he was concerned. ''I think you were simply expressing the point of view that I should take better care of myself.''

Thane shot her a grin. ''Exactly that.''

''And moreover,'' she stated, ''you're right. I should do a better job of cooking for myself, but I *can* make a mean casserole when the mood hits me.''

Meghan sipped the Stinger. And sipped again before adding more to the glass. She saw—but ignored—the look of disapproval Thane gave her as he ladled the last of the ingredients from the frying pan into the Dutch oven.

''If you'd allow me, I could show you how to butterfly a chop.'' He set the frying pan in the sink and walked back to stand beside her.

''You might be teaching me something I'll probably never use again,'' Meghan said.

''Then, again, in a wild and uncontrolled moment—when the mood hits—you might get the urge to butterfly a chop,'' Thane teased her.

She loved it when he teased her... or loved the smoldering sun look that came with the tease, she mused. In response to the look, she did feel an uncontrolled urge. Indeed she did. She was in the mood and amenable to any kind of demonstration the man had in mind, so slowly, never taking her gaze from Thane, she set her glass down. ''Okay,'' she said, ''demonstrate.''

Thane moved even closer, ignoring the three-foot limit. The enigma in her smile was coaxing him—but just in time, before he could slip his arm around her, he remembered he'd said platonic friendship, and he meant platonic.

He forced his gaze from hers, picked up the knife and said casually, "Watch carefully." He butterflied the chop. "That's it."

"That's it?" Meghan asked. She knew Thane had been debating whether or not to kiss her. She had to admit that she felt a stab of disappointment that she had come in second best to a cooking demonstration.

She quickly set the third chop in place, butterflied it, placed both butterflied chops and the one she'd mutilated into the Dutch oven with the other ingredients, then poured the sauerkraut over the meat.

In a short time the meal was in the oven. Together they did the dishes and wiped the counters, silently and deliberately avoiding contact of bodies and eyes.

As Meghan removed her apron and tossed it onto the cupboard, she glanced at the clock. Only two-and-a-half hours of silence and sipping the Stinger before they could eat.

"Well," Thane said. They were standing on opposite ends of the kitchen, and the silence was getting to him.

Meghan turned to face Thane. "Well what?"

Thane thought they were looking at each other with the bemused expression one sees in the eyes of lost sheep. "Well. What do we do now?"

The Stinger was gone from Meghan's glass. She gave herself a refill and with it came an absolutely brilliant idea. "Monopoly!"

"Monopoly?"

"Be back in a jiffy. We'll set up the board on the kitchen table." She scurried from the room.

"Murphy said the Donovans have eight Boston terrier pups," Thane said in a raised voice. Murphy had been with Meghan yesterday. He'd called from school asking permission to go to the Donovans with Chip and Doc to vaccinate and dock a litter of pups. Meghan had brought Murphy home in time for chores. She hadn't stayed. Thane had been in the farrowing house, so he hadn't seen her.

He carried their glasses to the table, pulled out a chair and sat. He was glad he'd thought of the Donovan pups. Dogs were a nice, safe, impersonal topic.

"They were a sweet bunch of pups," Meghan said as she entered the kitchen. She sat in the chair across the table from Thane, relieved to be talking—and dogs were a nice, safe topic. "Murphy loved the whole litter, one in particular."

"So I gathered," Thane said, settling back against the chair. "Murphy's convinced a Boston terrier is what we need to keep us company. Dad's Pekingese died last winter."

"A Boston terrier would make a good house dog," Meghan offered.

"I can visualize it now. I'm stretched on the sofa, resting—" The last time he'd been on the sofa he'd fallen asleep and dreamed Meghan was beside him running her fingers lightly around his navel, then woken to discover it was Finnigin's tail switching. He cleared his throat. "With a Boston terrier and Finnigin fighting for territorial rights to my chest," he concluded hastily, blushing mightily.

Meghan laughed, then quickly got busy setting up the board when the image he'd given her took a sensuous twist and she saw herself on his sofa with him. "Short or long game?" she questioned brightly.

"Short," Thane said just as brightly.

Meghan had finished the Stinger. She took time out to make a quick trip to the cupboard. So she wouldn't have to get up again, she brought the quart jar back to the table.

Two, maybe two-and-a-half glasses so far. She didn't want to overdo it. She was looking for a level of mellowness that would take the edge off the sexual sensations she was feeling. She hoped that state arrived before she was totally blitzed.

Chapter Eight

"When did you eat last?" Thane asked as Meghan refilled her glass.

"I don't know," she said.

"You don't know when you ate last?" he asked. Her eyes already had a vacant look. "Oh, brother."

"What does, 'oh, brother' mean?" Meghan asked, squinting and leaning forward.

"I said I wasn't going to warn you again, so just, oh, brother," Thane said.

"You sound like my brother, Shea," Meghan said. "He was always giving me vague warnings shrouded in doomsday tones."

"Did you ever take heed?" Thane asked.

"Occasionally." Meghan smiled.

Thane laughed. "I'll bet you did. Very occasionally. Shake the dice."

They played for half an hour, talking and laughing while Meghan kept sipping the brew, inching her way to lessening tension, which she finally achieved. She was feeling very comfortable with the good-looking, witty, charming Norseman sitting across the table from her. And as for those soft looks he gave her from time to time, well, she hadn't thrown herself into his arms—yet.

She decided to build houses on Marvin Gardens. "I'm buying one...no, two houses for Marvin Gardens," she said in a singsong voice as she picked up a house.

"You pay the bank first, Meghan. Then you take the houses. I doubt that you have the money, because a few minutes ago you bought the Electric Company from me for one thousand dollars. Remember?"

Meghan couldn't recall the transaction. "Wow! That seems pretty steep. Did you take advantage of me?" She leaned forward, peering at him. It was probably just an illusion, she thought, but he seemed to be moving farther and farther from the table. She started to take her houses over his silly protests about money.

"The telephone's ringing," Thane said.

"I heard it. I was 'bout to answer." Meghan attempted to stand, but her head took off in two different orbits and she settled back down on the chair. "Care to get it for me?"

Thane was gone and back before Meghan's brain had time to record the fact. "That was Murphy," he said.

It took a moment for her to locate Thane's body standing by the table, another to connect his voice to it. She smiled up at him.

"Blizzard warnings have been issued, so the Greers aren't taking the kids to the circus tonight. Murphy's staying overnight with them."

"No circus? Tha's too bad. Maybe we should call 'em and tell 'em t'come over. We could have a party," she suggested, reaching for her glass. "Now this—" she held the glass up as she admired the contents "—I'd like to have the reci-....reci-.... You know, Thane." She frowned. "The ingredients for."

Thane shook his head. Stung by the Stinger, he thought. "You're tipsy, my sweet lady. No more party for you tonight. And no more Stinger." He took the glass from her hand.

"I'm mel-low, my sweet man."

"Whatever you are, no more Stinger."

"Shouldn' I decide that?"

"Normally I'd agree. But you're in no shape to make the right decision. No, my dear girl. From here on in it's tomato juice and crackers for you."

"Tomato juice an' crackers! Wha' happened to supper?"

"Still cooking. I meant juice and crackers until the meal is ready," Thane said as he took the glass to the sink.

In a minute he was back, setting a glass of tomato juice and a bowl of crackers on the table. Meghan tilted her head to look up at him. With a fingertip he tenderly brushed the corner of her lip.

When she brought her hand up and caressed his fingers, he shuddered, raised her hand to his lips and kissed her fingertips, then guided her hand to the table, wrapped her fingers around the glass of tomato juice and ordered her, "Drink this, Meghan."

Meghan drank. Thane returned to his chair. He knew he should leave before the brunt of the storm arrived, but he couldn't leave Meghan in this condition. She had to be sober, or at least capable of putting herself in bed, because any thought of his helping her to bed was out of the question. There was a limit to his restraint!

The game continued for another hour.

The effects of the Stinger Meghan had consumed wore off to the point where she realized how plowed she'd been and was thoroughly embarrassed. "I want to apologize for not listening to you, Thane. Really, my behavior tonight has been unforgivable.''

"You've got nothing to apologize for, Meghan. My being here without Murphy made you edgy, so you indulged. And on an empty stomach it's no wonder the Stinger hit you like it did," Thane said.

"I like the way you make excuses for me," Meghan said sincerely. She failed to roll doubles, and she'd remain in jail, because she didn't have the money to post bail. For all intents and purposes, the game was over. "Thanks for taking the Stinger away from me," she added as she gave him the dice.

"All in the line of friendship," Thane said, his voice low.

"How *are* we doing on the friendship thing, anyway? Did anything exciting happen while I was being mellow?"

Thane laughed. "You did try to build a motel on Baltic Avenue."

"I did? I don't own Baltic Avenue."

"Exactly. But I had a hell of a time trying to convince you of that.... Meghan, why didn't you ever marry?"

She met his almond gaze across the expanse of table. Why *hadn't* she married? Of one thing she was sure. It was because the right man hadn't come along. "I'd never had reason to give marriage much thought," she said honestly.

"You must have had offers of marriage."

"Yes. There were offers, but never from—" Meghan was saying when the telephone rang again. "Darn it. Excuse me." She stood, and the room did a slow spin. She steadied herself by spreading her palms on the table for a moment, then moved to the phone.

A minute later, she returned the receiver to the cradle and turned to see Thane putting the Monopoly set away. "I have to go into the country," she said. "Leroy Blanchard has a cow down. Possible pneumonia. He's given the cow an antibiotic, but she hasn't responded. He wondered if I'd check her. From the directions he gave me, I understand he lives north and east of your place."

"I heard," Thane said. This is the way it would always be with Meghan, he thought. A phone call interrupting an evening or an important conversation. "I haven't seen Leroy for a while. It'll be good to see him."

"What do you mean it'll be good to see him?"

"I'm going with you."

"I'd assumed you'd either go home or stay here until I got back."

"You assumed wrong. The roads will be bad," Thane said, looking up to meet the challenge in her voice.

"I've driven on bad roads through Kansas blizzards."

"Not tipsy, you haven't."

"I'm sober," she retorted. Thane pressed his lips together, looking stern. She amended, "Almost."

"I'm going. And not only am I going, but I'm driving. I know that twisting gravel road leading to Leroy's. Now, that's my last word on it. I have my coveralls, overshoes and parka in the pickup. I'll change and be ready to leave when you are." He was already moving toward the door.

"You're ordering me around, and I'm not sure I like it. And besides, there's no reason for you to feel you should go with me, Thane."

"There's a reason, all right," Thane said as he turned to confront her. "If I don't go with you, I'd worry myself sick wondering how you were negotiating that road leading to Leroy's. I'd have visions of the pickup in the ditch, overturned or slammed into a tree. Get the picture?"

"I get the picture. You're going with me," Meghan said. Again he'd won the argument by expressing his concern for her well-being. That knowledge mellowed her beyond all reason, beyond the ability of any home brew called the Stinger.

* * *

Thane peered through the windshield and into the snow, which was being whirled across the road in a series of white tornadoes. The headlights of the pickup penetrated only a few feet into the blowing snow before bouncing back a sickly-looking yellow. Fireflies would have given better lighting, he thought. For all practical purposes, he was driving blindly.

"It must have snowed another inch or two while we were at Leroy's," he said.

"The way the wind's forcing the snow at us, it's hard to tell," Meghan said, keeping her eyes pinned on the right side of the road. When she spotted a clump of brome or the fence line, she warned Thane they were close to the ditch.

"I'm beginning to think we should have accepted Leroy's invitation to spend the night," Thane said. He was responsible, because he'd told Leroy that things weren't that bad and that they'd have no trouble getting back into town.

"Watch it!" Meghan yelled. Thane swung the steering wheel left. Bucking through a drift, the pickup reared and settled. She glanced at Thane, who frowned in concentration. Her gaze drifted to his hands, to the grip of his fingers on the wheel.

"It was nice meeting Leroy's bride," she offered.

"Interesting situation, there," Thane said. "Leroy says the minute he and Sally saw each other they knew they were in love. I hope it works out for them, but a month isn't long to know someone before making a lifetime commitment."

"Don't sound so pessimistic, Thane," Meghan said as she strained to see the ditch. Nothing out there but blackness and white fingers furiously trying to break the glass of the window... for a flash she recalled another night like this. Riding through a blizzard with her father...

"I'm being realistic, Meghan," Thane said. He muttered something when the pickup collided with another drift.

Once through it, he said, "Reason argues against the marriage. Leroy was a bachelor who'd never dated anyone on a regular basis. Now he's married to a woman half his age."

"Half his age and quite beautiful," Meghan added, thankful Thane had kept talking. The anxiety that had come over her when she recalled the accident she and her father had had was fleeting.

"Sally's beautiful, all right," Thane agreed. "Which only makes me wonder more if Leroy's been around enough to know the difference between love and infatuation."

"You don't believe in meaningful gazes sent across a crowded room?" Meghan asked. If he said no, he'd be hedging, she knew. The gazes they'd exchanged tonight hadn't lost intensity even while she worked with Leroy's cow, Thane watching.

"Oh, I believe in meaningful gazes, all right," Thane said dryly. "But I also believe few people know the difference between love at first sight and physical entrapment. At least I didn't with Cassandra."

Meghan kept her eyes to the right, looking for the ditch. Thane sounded so bitter, so hurt. Entrapment. Was that what he felt when he looked at her, too? Didn't he believe in love anymore?

"I can tell you why Sally was and is attracted to Leroy," she said. "He's soft-spoken, sincere, and he has beautiful, warm sea-green eyes that make you forget his age and his balding head."

"Warm, sea-green? Really!"

"My goodness, Thane. That sounded testy. Wouldn't happen to be a bit jealous, would you?" Meghan prodded, hoping he was. She didn't care if she was being coy or adolescent. Just once she wanted Thane to admit he was struggling to maintain his calm demeanor.

"I'm not jealous. I'm impressed that you saw Leroy for what he is, a gentle soul." Thane leaned forward, squinting. "I can't see a damn thing. How about you, Meghan?"

"Nothing. Nothing at all." She tightened her grip on the dashboard. "How beautiful do you think Sally is?" she asked.

"Beautiful is beautiful when it comes to another man's wife—good grief! Look at that wind blow!" Thane had the pickup barely inching along. Much slower and they might as well be stopped, he thought.

"You're evading the question, MacDougal. Is it Sally's beauty that you don't trust?"

"She's a beautiful woman with an intriguing smile," Thane said. "And I don't distrust her. I only hope she understands she's married to a farmer, whose life-style is more sitting on the front porch swinging than it is rocking and rolling at the country club. One thing's for sure—it's not as exciting as some women would like."

"I think farming and ranching are wild and exciting," Meghan said. "Just breathing the air is an invigorating experience."

Thane laughed. "Especially around the hog yards."

"You bet. Especially there." She laughed.

"By the way," Thane said, "I'm with a more beautiful woman than Sally right now. One whose smile intrigues me more than Sally's does."

Meghan turned her head to focus on Thane's handsome profile. She'd always taken her looks for what they were: good on a good day. But never *beautiful* in the classical, porcelain-skinned, perfect-featured way Sally was. Yet just as Thane had made her feel utterly feminine the day she'd been stuck in the barnyard, now he made her feel utterly beautiful. And if he thought her smile was intriguing, she'd smile at him often—

"Meghan," Thane said. "I can't look to see what you're doing, but I feel you looking at me and not watching for the ditch."

"I'm looking—" Meghan's gaze flew back to her given duty. A barbed fence! "Pull it over fast!" she screamed. Thane jerked the steering wheel left. "More! We're still too—"

As the steering wheel was jerked from Thane's grasp, Meghan was pitched forward, then thrown back by her seat belt. The cutting tightness of the belt over her stomach and chest took her breath away. She groaned, not from physical pain but from the pain of the memory that had surfaced for the second time tonight.

Thane bounced forward, then back. "Were you saying we were too close to the ditch? I'll amend that to we're *in* the ditch. And stuck. You okay, Meghan?" he asked.

"Yes. Fine. But are you sure we're stuck?" Meghan stared straight ahead. She was trying to keep out of her voice the swell of panic she was feeling. She'd thought she'd put that horror behind her.

"We settled like a sinker in water, but I'll see what I can do." Thane threw the pickup into reverse, shifted into forward. "We're not going anywhere in this pickup, Meghan. My place is about half a mile from here. We'll walk."

"Walk? I—it's so cold."

She was joking, Thane thought. She was accustomed to the cold, to sharp winds, to snow whipping her face. Her body, though soft and feminine, had the muscle tone of an athlete's. He unsnapped his seat belt.

"This is Iowa in March. Seventy balmy degrees one day and five with snow the next," he said, turning toward her to discover she hadn't even made a move to unbuckle herself; she was still and looked pale. "You did get hurt, didn't you?" he asked, alarmed.

"No. No, I'm fine. I just don't want to walk."

Thane's alarm grew when Meghan turned toward him, her eyes wide and wild. He edged across the seat, unlocked her seat belt, then slipped his arm over her shoulder and took her trembling hand into his. "Did you bang your head, Meghan?" he asked, nudging her chin up to direct the focus of her eyes into his.

She blinked. "No. I told you. I... don't want to walk."

"The walk won't be a pleasant one, but there's nothing to fear," he said. He nuzzled the side of her head, listening to her shallow, quick breathing. Her hands were like ice. She was on the verge of panic.

"I'm being unreasonable," she whispered.

"You aren't being unreasonable," he assured her. "Tell me why you're afraid." He wanted to tighten his hold on her, kiss her until she forgot whatever had caused her fear, but he sensed what she needed from him was to be held. He pressed her shaking body to his, stroked her hand.

"I've been through a dozen nights like this since the accident," she said, stumbling over the words, knowing she wasn't making sense. "I... Just give me a minute to compose myself."

Thane squeezed her shoulder. The only sounds in the cab came from the wheezing of the wind trying to force its way through small cracks, from the sluggish whisk of the windshield wipers. He eased his right hand to the back of her neck and began kneading her knotted muscles.

Finally the gentle touch of Thane's hands, the reassuring feel of her body tucked next to his, gave Meghan the courage to confront the emotions that had disabled her.

"I almost killed Dad on a night like this," she said. When she turned her eyes to Thane's, he nodded in encouragement and touched her ear. She nestled her head trustingly on his shoulder.

"I was fourteen at the time. Dad had taken me into town so I could get my learner's permit. While we were in town it began raining and the rain turned to snow. In spite of the weather I teased Dad to allow me to drive home—which isn't as stupid as it sounds. I'd been driving on the ranch for a couple of years.''

"I understand," Thane said softly. "I was behind the wheel of a tractor by the time I was Murphy's age."

Meghan sighed. "I'll bet you don't give in to Murphy's teasing to drive a tractor, do you?"

"No. I remember coming close to tipping a tractor over when I was about twelve. It scared me enough so I'm firm in telling Murphy that he can't drive until he's old enough to understand the power he has under hand."

"Maybe daughters are different from sons. Dad could never refuse me when I teased. So that evening as we headed out of town I was driving. And Dad kept telling me to slow it down, because the roads were icy. I laughed. 'Dad,' I told him. 'Trust me. I've got things under control.'"

She took a deep breath. "I hit an icy patch on the road. The pickup flipped and skidded down the highway. The next thing I remember was hanging upside down with the steering wheel jammed into my stomach."

She turned her head on Thane's shoulder and was met with a sympathetic gaze. She looked away. She didn't have understanding coming. "I managed to free myself, but Dad was unconscious. Bleeding from the nose. I wanted to stay with him. I...was afraid he was dying. But I had to get help. I left him. I was blinded by snow. I wandered from the road several times...."

Thane brushed his lips over her temple. She was trembling. "It must have been a terrifying experience for a child of fourteen."

"I was petrified. It was dumb luck that I found a house."

"But you did find help."

"Yes. But Dad spent a week in the hospital with broken ribs and a concussion—all because I was so blasted cocky."

Thane brushed her temple with his lips again and this time allowed himself a lingering feel of the delicate texture of her skin. He whispered against her cheek, "Sure. You were cocky. And you teased. But it was your father who made the decision to allow you to drive and the decision to allow you to keep driving. If he'd thought you were really going too fast, he would have made you stop the pickup so he could drive."

"*I* rolled that pickup, Thane. Dad didn't."

"The accident happened, Meghan. And maybe it shouldn't have, but most fourteen-year-olds would have panicked and stayed in the pickup, watching helplessly, rather than challenging a blizzard alone. In my eyes, your walking for help was heroic. Meghan..." He forgot what he'd intended to say. They'd been too close for too long, and his thoughts were turning away from comforting to seeing how deep and dreamy her eyes were in the pale light coming from the dashboard. "You do take risks without regard for your personal safety. Tonight when Leroy called, you didn't hesitate to say you'd come out."

"And I risked *your* neck along with mine! You could have been killed!" Meghan said, then felt the rumbling of Thane's laughter in his chest. She looked up at him. "Why are you laughing? You could have been. And I don't find having your death on my conscience funny!"

"Meghan! You're priceless. You know we weren't going fast enough to get killed."

Meghan felt like a total wreck. Thane's gaze was teasing her, and she felt weepy. He'd told her she was priceless—and she wanted to blubber like a baby.

"I was responsible for you being with me," she insisted. "If you'd been killed—if Dad had been killed—"

"Now that's enough, Meghan," Thane said. "I made the decision to come with you. I told you I knew the road and look where I put us—in the ditch."

"I wasn't watching for the ditch. I was looking at you," Meghan admitted.

"And I was feeling darn good knowing you were looking at me, even though I knew you should be watching for the ditch." Thane ran his fingers over the outline of her trembling lips. "What do you think of that?"

Thane was saying all the right things to comfort her, shifting the responsibility for their predicament from her shoulders to his. He was so blessed understanding and tolerant, she thought. Why did he have to be so narrow-minded when it came to her career?

"Oh," Meghan groaned. "I think I'm going to cry."

Thane feathered a touch over her cheek, touched the moisture gathering in the corner of her eye. "So cry, sweet Meghan."

"But . . . why should I cry?" Meghan asked, already sniffling. Dammit. She never cried without a reason. "I didn't even cry the night I thought I'd killed Dad."

"Cry—it'll release the tension you've been under all night," Thane crooned. "And cry for the little girl who didn't cry the night her dad was hurt because she had to face the bigger challenge of saving his life."

"Oh, Thane—keep holding me?"

"I won't let you go," Thane assured her.

Meghan cried until her chest and throat ached and her eyes burned from the hot tears. She took a deep, steadying breath. "This is worse than the onion," she said, using her fingers to wipe away the tears. "But I do feel better."

Thane reached inside his coveralls and came out with a huge red farmer's handkerchief. He put his fingers under her chin and turned her face to him, dabbing at her cheeks, her eyes, before he lowered the handkerchief and kissed her tear-wet lips. When she began to respond, to reach for him, his body scalded and he broke off the kiss.

"There I go," he said hoarsely, "breaking the rules. Getting closer than three feet." He stuffed the handkerchief in his pocket. "We do have to walk, Meghan."

Chapter Nine

Meghan nodded. "I'm fine now. Really."

Thane zipped her coveralls to her neck, pulled her parka closed and zipped it, then took her ski mask from her pocket and slid it on over her hair, then down over her face. Once the mask was in place, he smiled.

"What are you smiling at?" she asked.

"The mask pushes your nose in, and your eyes have kind of a staring look. You remind me of an owl," Thane said. When he saw the smile on her lips—as it showed through the mask's lip slit—settle in her eyes, he slid away and zipped his parka.

Meghan pulled her parka hood up and snapped it into place and slipped her gloves on. After Thane had settled his hood in place, turned the pickup off, slipped on his gloves and was reaching to turn the lights off, she got the flashlight out of the glove compartment and handed it to him.

He surprised her by laughing. "Don't tell me! With no debate at all you're going to let me be the leader?"

"I'm going to give you a second chance to show me that you really do know the road," Meghan said.

"In that case, let's go." He turned on the flashlight and forced the door open.

The storm roared into the cab on a freezing scream. Meghan slid across the seat and stepped out into hip-deep snow.

"I have never been so cold," Meghan yelled even though Thane was no more than a foot ahead of her. Her teeth were chattering, her nose numb under her ski mask.

They'd encountered another waist-high drift not ten feet from the pickup. Since then Meghan had lost count of the drifts Thane had plowed through before reaching back to help her.

"If you're tiring, hang on to my parka. We're nearly to the lane."

Meghan did as he suggested, dipping her head behind the fortress of his broad shoulders to give her face a break from the wind, which seared down her throat to scorch her lungs. "How long before we get there?" she hollered.

"Murphy used to ask that question every time we got into a car. Of course, he was only a couple of years old at the time," Thane said. He felt Meghan give him a little shove in the back. "If you're feeling that frisky, Meghan, how about you breaking the path for a while?"

"Ha!"

"That's what I thought." Thane raised his hand to shield his face from a blast of wind while he tried to check their position. In a strange and wonderful way, he wasn't feeling cold. Meghan's closeness was holding the intense cold at bay.

"Hey! You!" he called.

"What?"

"I was just thinking there's no one I'd rather walk with through a blizzard than you."

"Why?"

"You aren't begging me to carry you." He was moving head down, following gut feelings about where they were, where they were going.

"Some compliment!" Meghan said. "I was expecting something romantic." The shove Meghan gave him this time brought an explosion of air from his lungs.

"You're living dangerously, Meghan."

"I don't want to discuss it. How long *have* we been walking? You said we only had to go half a mile. Are you sure you know where you're going?"

Thane laughed. "A minute ago I was thinking what a trooper you were not to be complaining. I was saying to myself, 'Man. You're lucky. Other women would be complaining along about now. But not old Meghan. She's a trooper.'"

"You're full of it, Thane. I'm not complaining. I'm frozen. Even my knees are stiff."

Thane made his way through another drift, then turned to give Meghan a hand. "Apparently the freezing condition you're suffering from hasn't reached your mouth," he said before wheeling to face the blowing snow again.

"*That* wasn't nice, Thane."

"But it *was* true."

"Thane?"

"Yes, Meghan."

"If something happened to me, would you carry me?"

"You know I couldn't carry you," Thane yelled. The wind took his breath away.

"Would you try?"

"Hell, yes, I'd try. And we'd both end up frozen. Does that thought make you happy?"

"Yes. That makes me happy." Thane made her happy. Walking—struggling—through the storm together made her happy. Maybe she *had* taken a blow to the head when the pickup went into the ditch. The piercing wind suddenly felt like a gentle April shower. The smell of wildflowers floated on the air. "Yes," she reiterated. "That makes me happy."

"Happy we'd freeze?" Thane asked.

"No. Happy that you'd try to carry me rather than leave me behind." Suddenly she wanted to be at the house, where she could catch more than the occasional glimpse of his face she got when he turned to pull her through a drift. "Can't you move any faster?"

"*I* could move faster, but you're hanging on to my coat-tail."

"You told me to hang on," Meghan reminded him.

"That I did."

They were at the back porch steps and climbing before Meghan realized that they'd crossed Thane's yard and that they were at the house steps and not another snow drift.

"I'd begun to think we'd never get here," Meghan said, stamping her feet. She began brushing at the snow that clung to her parka and coverall legs.

"Don't worry about the snow. We'll brush off inside." Thane opened the door and drew Meghan through as he switched on the mudroom light. After shutting the door, he turned to look at her.

"You look like a snow woman," he said. "With the quizzical black eyes of an owl."

Meghan pulled her gloves off. "Big deal, MacDougal. You look like a Sasquatch."

"There's no such beast," he said, thinking her lips were apple red and looked succulent, inviting a taste.

"I've seen pictures. They even have a golden mane and beard like yours, those Sasquatch," Megan insisted, grinning.

"I like my beard." Thane grabbed a broom. "Turn your back to me." Snickering, she turned. Thane brushed the snow from her parka. Brisk over the shoulders, slower over the buttocks. Then, when she least suspected it, he caught the backs of her knees with it, causing her to crumple before he caught her under her arm and righted her.

"Just checking to see if your knees were really frozen in place." He chuckled. "The snow is packed. Hold still." He whacked the backs of her knees again.

She tossed him a warning glance over her shoulder, but her eyes were deep and luminous, so her threat lost something in flight. "Done in back. Turn," he ordered. "I'll get the front."

Meghan dropped the parka hood and pulled the ski mask from her head as she pivoted to face him. "Are you getting a big kick from smacking me with that broom?" she asked, fluffing her hair with her fingers.

"I am. Who did all the work as a snowplow, and who kept pushing me in the back? And then who called me a Sasquatch, instead of thanking me for saving her sweet life?" he asked. He started brushing again.

Meghan was standing on a rug, but the snow Thane was whisking away was flying all over the mudroom floor. "There's going to be a puddle, my sweet man."

"That's what mudrooms are for," he said. Her cheeks were turning rosy. *My sweet man,* he thought. How he loved hearing those words coming from her lips—even in teasing. "Arms up," he ordered brusquely.

Meghan raised her arms over head, concentrating on his face as he swiped under her arms with the tip of the bristles. "I may have given you a few tiny shoves," she said, "but you can't blame me because you look like Big Foot."

Thane grinned and didn't temper the delivery of the bristles over her abdomen. With her intake of air he announced, "Done."

"My turn," Meghan said, thinking of revenge as she took the broom from his hand. "Backside first," she said sweetly.

Thane stepped onto the rug and turned, knowing from the gleeful glint in her eyes that she was going to belt him. He also knew she couldn't do any damage. "How's this?" he asked as he raised his arms above his heads.

"Oh, that's perfect!" Meghan stepped back, choked up on the broom handle and delivered the bristles behind his knees with the same swing she'd used to help her college softball team win a championship.

Thane's hands flew out so he could catch himself on the wall. "Dammit, Meghan! I didn't hit you that hard."

"Yes, you did. Don't grumble. Think of it this way—now we're even for you pushing me into Diller's freezer." She moderated the brushing over the rest of his legs and covered the expanse of his back in firm downward strokes.

"I did not push you into that freezer, Miss Forester. You know I didn't!"

"Don't argue. Turn," she said.

"You brandish that broom as if you had experience," Thane said when he was facing her.

"You bet. I'm an old hand at this brushing off. It was survival of the fittest when my brother, sister and I squared off." She whirled the broom like a sword, then attacked.

He uttered a real protest. "I never hit you there!"

"You know you did."

"Not that hard."

"Hard enough."

"You'd better stop swinging at me like that, or I'll have to take your broom-brushing privileges away from you," Thane threatened, feigning a sinister look.

"Oh, please. No!" Meghan said, pretending to cower and whimper.

Thane deteriorated into a fit of laughter, with Meghan joining him. And by the time they had completed the snow removal, removed their parkas, coveralls and overshoes, he was weakened but experiencing the same feeling of well-being he got from running three miles.

All right, he admitted to himself as he stepped into the kitchen and turned the light on, his good feeling came from being with Meghan. Warm house or snowstorm, Meghan was the difference between the blahs and feeling wonderful.

"If you're still frozen, I suggest a warm bath in the tub upstairs," he said when Meghan joined him.

Bath! Meghan's mind screamed. Thane's expression was innocent of anything but concern—but they were together. Alone. Isolated from the world. She couldn't take a bath in *his* tub. "I think...a blanket will warm me," she said.

"What's the matter? Don't you trust me, Meghan?"

"Believe me, I trust you, Thane. It's me that I don't trust. I'm afraid I might forget the ground rules of this friendship. I might ask if sharing the sofa is permissible. I might even ask if a kiss is permissible." Would her teasing voice fool him while she made the admission?

"You wouldn't," Thane said.

"I might."

Thane was dead in the water in spite of her shamming seriousness. His mind was in revolt. He wanted to kiss her—she was so easy to love. Why was he fighting it?

"Are you thinking about trying to seduce me?" he asked.

"Could you be seduced?" she asked.

"Highly likely."

The drop in the tone of his voice, the deepening glow in his eyes, caused Meghan to quake with anticipation. She was tempted. Thane's desire for her was etched on his face, manifest in his gaze. But what would come of seduction but complications neither could deal with in the harsh light of day?

"You still aren't scaring me, Thane," Meghan said slowly. "But I've scared myself. I do so want to be in your arms, kissing you, and what frightens me is that I don't feel the least bit ashamed to admit it. Nor the least bit ashamed to admit I've never felt this way about another man.''

"I find I'm in the same perplexing position," Thane whispered, reaching for her.

Meghan shook her head and inched away. "We've been through an ordeal. We aren't thinking straight. The expedient thing for me to do is accept your thoughtful offer to warm myself in your tub and make a quick and dignified exit.''

"Expedient? Out of concern for yourself or for me?'' Thane asked, stepping toward her.

"You, of course," Meghan said, moving into an area of darkness between the kitchen and the front room. "I wouldn't want to compromise your position on what you believe is the right woman for you, Thane.''

Meghan knew she sounded bolder than she felt; acted more in control than she was. She had no doubt that if he followed her into the shadowy darkness she would flow toward him like melted butter.

"I'm not so sure my position would be compromised," Thane said in a strangled voice.

"Well, I'm not sure you'd be compromised, either, but I still think the wise thing for me to do is to warm myself in the tub." Before she could change her mind, follow her body's screaming demand for a sensual warming, she fled upstairs.

Thane resisted the temptation to call Meghan back. She was right. It was wise and it was expedient, but dammit, she wanted him and he wanted her. So what would be so wrong about acting on their needs? This noble experiment of being friends was torture. And what were they gaining from it?

Get busy, MacDougal. Take your mind off knowing that the snow and the night winds have locked the world out— and you and Meghan in. Start a fire in the fireplace. Take a shower. Fix a lunch. Meghan must be starved. At least he wasn't being driven out of his mind wondering where she was.

Would she be slipping from her shirt as she drew the bathwater, or would she take off her jeans first? Maybe he should go up and see if she'd found the towels. As tired as she was, she could fall asleep in the tub. Maybe he should go up—to rescue her.

Maybe he shouldn't. What did he think, that he was Casanova reincarnated? That once loved by him, she would *see* that she needed him—that some things she couldn't do alone? Hell, he was a heel!

The first thing Meghan saw when she came downstairs after her bath was that Thane had made a fire. She was drawn to it and, once there, stood before the hearth with her hands extended to the warmth. She yawned. The bath had sapped her of energy. Her nose twitched. Besides the aroma of the burning wood, she smelled cocoa. Then the impolite growling of her stomach reminded her how hungry she was.

She turned from the fireplace, walked to the kitchen and paused in the doorway. Thane was taking sandwich makings from the refrigerator and setting them on the center counter. His golden hair was damp and curly from his shower. He'd dressed in a navy sweater and faded jeans. Remarkable, she thought, no matter the color or cut of the clothes, he looked sexy. No other word so accurately described his physical makeup.

Instead of standing in the doorway mooning over him, she told herself, she should offer to help him make the sandwiches just as he'd helped— "Oh, my goodness! The sauerkraut and trimmings."

With the sound of Meghan's voice, Thane felt a rush of erotic arousal but when he turned to see her eyes darkened with weariness, he could only think she needed food, then a good night's sleep.

"I turned it off before we left."

Meghan nodded. She covered her mouth with her hand when she felt a yawn coming on. "I'm sorry, Thane. It isn't your company causing me to yawn." She laughed, and the laugh turned into yet another huge yawn.

"Why don't you rest on the sofa while I throw these sandwiches together? Cheese and sliced beef okay with you? Whole wheat or rye?" Thane asked with businesslike briskness.

"Whole wheat. And I love beef and cheese. If you have any marshmallows to go with the cocoa, I could handle a few dozen. I'm famished."

"Love to see a woman with a healthy appetite. Now, go rest."

"Thane, if I sit, I won't be awake to eat. All you've done tonight is take care of me. You fixed supper, sobered me from my mellow state," she said, grinning, then added seriously, "and comforted me before pulling me through one snowdrift after another."

"I can't remember ever enjoying myself as much as I have tonight, Meghan," Thane said.

"Me, either," Meghan said. His gaze was on her, probing and unwavering, as she walked to the center counter where he was working. "But I don't think it would be wise of me to get into the habit of having you take care of me, so I'm going to help with the sandwiches. What do you want me to do?"

Thane opened the mayonnaise. "If you insist on helping, slice the beef. And don't butterfly it."

"Cute, Thane. Thin slices or thick?" she asked, picking up the knife Thane had placed on the chopping block. "*This* is a butcher knife," she said.

Thane laughed. Clearly she was exhausted, but her sense of humor was intact. "You're a fast learner," he said. "Thin slices. Pickles?"

"Can't have a sandwich without them." Meghan had never been so tired physically, and yet she was filled with a mind-consuming joy. She wanted to sing. Dance. Be crazy. First the feeling of April in a March blizzard, and now this! She wanted to put Thane in her sweater pocket like a good-luck charm and keep him with her forever.

"Mustard and lettuce?" he asked.

"That's my man." Meghan sliced the beef. Without looking up, she asked, "Thane?"

"What?"

"Oh . . . forget it." Meghan sliced another piece of beef.

"Don't do that to me, Meghan. If you want to ask a question, ask it."

"Um...well. I really don't like to think of myself as being so independent that I can take on the world single-handed. It isn't that I can't," she hastened to explain as their gazes met over the counter. "It's only that it would be nice to have someone to share my life with."

"I know what you mean," Thane said.

"But that wasn't what I was going to say," Meghan said. "I was going to ask you a question." She sliced another piece of beef, gaze cast determinedly down.

Thane picked the beef up and stacked it on the prepared bread. She was acting strange, and when she looked up there was a strange look in her expression. Maybe she'd had a knock in the head. First the drowsiness, and now this. But her pupils weren't extremely dilated, only very black, soft and inviting.

"Well," he said. "I'm waiting for the question."

"Well...what I was wondering was...what do you think the chances are that we're falling in love?"

"Damn!" he exploded. "Look at what I did to this bread!"

"Why, you put your fingerprints in it," Meghan assessed, then looked up at him with a smile that was only partially teasing. "Does the thought of falling in love with me upset you that much?"

"Two things need to be said here," Thane said. "First—that was hardly the kind of question I expected to hear coming from you. Second—I'm trying to put a damper on the fire in my guts, which isn't easy to do when you keep fanning the embers."

Meghan swept her hands through the air in a gesture of utter frustration. "Oh, tell me about it! I suppose you think you're easy on me. The difference between us is that I, rather than trying to evade the issue, am willing to admit the possibility that we're falling in love and decide what to do about it. Do we go forward or retreat?"

"Ye gods, Meghan. Your approach isn't exactly conventional. Next topic on the agenda. Love. The possibilities of and the decisions available. To plunge or not to plunge headlong into love—that is the question!" He picked up two slices of bread.

"Was that your best attempt at being sarcastically evasive?" Meghan asked. She placed her hand on the counter and leaned forward until her nose was only inches away from him.

Thane narrowed his eyes. He wasn't letting her get to him that way—putting her lips within inches of his! "Yes, it was my best attempt."

"Too bad. So answer the question, because I've been reserved all my life when it came to men, and to this point what it's gotten me is nothing." She straightened, placing her hands on her hips. "What do you think the chances are that we're falling in love?"

"Give me a minute to consider the idea." Thane spread mayonnaise on the bread.

"One thousand one, one thousand two—"

"All right," Thane said. He looked up, his expression hard. "The question really should be, do you have time to fall in love, Meghan? You're stretched to the limits of your endurance right now. You've taken on a new business in a new town, and the first time I asked you for a date you didn't have time—"

"I asked for a rain check," Meghan interrupted.

"But at the time you didn't have time. Now, what makes you believe you have time to fall in love with me?" Thane demanded.

"If you have to ask a question like that, then you're comparing me with Cassandra," Meghan retorted, thinking how easily she and Thane flew at each other. "Because Cassandra had a career and didn't have time for you and Murphy, you won't consider the possibility that I could be a wife, mother and veterinarian." She sighed, sliced another piece of beef. "Will this be enough beef?"

"I think so," Thane said. "The only way you remind me of Cassandra is careerwise, Meghan."

Meghan wondered if she should thank him for telling her that. No. She wasn't sure he'd intended to be complimentary. She wrapped up the remaining roast, took the knife to the sink, turned and leaned against the counter.

"Am I wrong to want it all, Thane? If not with you, then someone else?" She couldn't conceive of it being anyone else.

She sure knew how to get to him, Thane thought. Someone else! Unthinkable. But him? Equally unthinkable. "No. You aren't wrong. The problem isn't with you, Meghan." He glanced over his shoulder. "It's with me. I know that. I couldn't handle knowing I wasn't as important to you as your work."

Meghan stalked back to the counter and planted herself directly across from Thane, then waited until his gaze met hers. "That is *bunk*, and you know it. Being a veterinarian is—"

"A real and powerful love for you," Thane injected. "And, as the saying goes, a demanding lover. I know myself, Meghan. If I fell in love with you and you returned my love, I'd be a demanding lover. I'd be selfish, jealous of the time you spent with that *other* lover."

"What if I said you could share me with my work?" Meghan offered enticingly.

"That would be a solution." Thane moved away to stir the cocoa. When he looked at her he wasn't reasonable; he believed he could share her with her career. "Unfortunately, I'm not capable of sharing your affections."

"Well, talk about unfair," Meghan sputtered. "You can't know that until you've tried it."

"I have tried it," Thane said harshly. "We're at an impasse. You can't give up your work. I wouldn't ask you to. Offhand I'd say you'd be a fool to fall in love with me and I'd be a fool to fall in love with you."

He walked back to stand across the counter from her. "Tell me I'm right, Meghan. Admit that we shouldn't fall in love."

The muscles in Meghan's jaw tightened. He was imploring her. So he'd tried it. But not with her. "No. We can't be at an impasse," she said. "If we care for each other and if there's a chance it could develop into love, then there must be a way to work this through."

Thane's gaze made her feel as if she were dancing to a torch song. She was trembling from desire and frustration. "Thane, we aren't children playing in a sandbox, saying to each other, 'Play the way I want to play or I won't be your friend,'" she insisted.

"We aren't children," Thane agreed. "But sometimes we act like children. And I'm starting to think one of the most childish ideas we've had so far was thinking we could be friends and nothing more. It wasn't only childish; it was a stupid idea."

"Aha!" Meghan responded heatedly. "Being friends was *your* idea! And I don't think it was stupid. But, Thane, where do we go from here?"

"I told you. I don't know." Thane piled the sandwiches on a plate.

"Do you want to call the friendship off?" Meghan asked, fearing that in his present mood he would say yes.

"I need thinking time before I try to answer that one. Let's eat in the front room, by the fire."

There were times for thinking. And Meghan agreed this was one of them. What neither had said but what both knew was that they had reached the point where their friendship was in jeopardy.

Chapter Ten

As they ate, Thane sitting in the overstuffed chair and Meghan on the sofa, by mutual agreement they talked about everything but the status of their friendship. At first the subjects were far-reaching in scope, from how pending farm legislation would affect the small farmer to the schedule offering of the Sioux City symphony orchestra, before they began exchanging tales of school days and childhood memories.

Thane settled back in his chair, smiling. Meghan had just finished telling him how she'd broken Shea's nose because he wouldn't stop teasing her about her very first boyfriend. She hadn't been able to get Shea to stop, so she'd balled a fist, closed her eyes and let fly.

He was chuckling one moment, thinking, I can see her swinging, and the next staring humorlessly at the flames of the fire. If it could always be like this. Quiet times with Meghan. Times to get to know each other. Thane glanced at her, then away. He felt the warmth flowing from the crackling fire but knew that the greater, more haunting warmth flooding through his veins came directly from that brief glance at Meghan. Haunting because the feeling had nothing to do with sensual sensations.

He hadn't known how lonely his life had been until he met her. If he could only justify going forward, find reasons it would work for them.

Meghan set her cocoa aside. "What does that distant look in your eyes mean, Thane?" she asked. "Something you could tell a friend?"

Thane chuckled and crossed one leg over the other, still gazing at the fire. "Yes, it's something I can tell a friend. I was wondering how your family spent the holidays when you were a child."

Meghan smiling, pulled off her cowboy boots and drew her legs onto the sofa before answering. "Usually my grandparents and a bundle of aunts and uncles with a gang of kids came to the ranch. We kids ran wild while the adults visited. Big dinner. Game playing. Loving and loud about says it."

Meghan leaned her head back on the sofa, glancing at Thane before turning her gaze to the fireplace. "What about you?"

Thane looked from the flames of Meghan's hair to the flames in the fireplace. "Quiet would describe holidays best. Christmas. Thanksgiving. Birthdays. All quiet. Dad was an only child. One of mother's sisters lived on the west coast, the other in Canada."

When Thane fell still, Meghan glanced at him. He was stroking his beard thoughtfully. "Quiet times are good, too," she ventured.

Thane sensed her gaze on him, and he looked at her. Her eyes were soft, luminous. "Believe me, I understand that now, but as a kid I was envious when friends began talking about who was coming for Christmas dinner. I was even envious of Tina and Bill. There were times when I resented them for having brothers and sisters. And a moment ago, even while I was vicariously enjoying myself listening to you describe punching out Shea—and how holidays were for you as a child—I was envious of you, of your relationship with your family.''

The dropping of a burned log into the fire drew Thane's attention. He rose, used the poker to rearrange the logs, then added another to the blaze before returning to his chair.

Meghan finished her cocoa and sat toying with the rim of the cup. Her heart was breaking for the child Thane. For the man Thane, who couldn't find the woman who could help him make his dream of family come true. And maybe her heart was breaking for herself.

"You're talking about Murphy, too, aren't you," she said. "Thinking he's missing something by not having a full-time mother, sisters and brothers, and blaming yourself for not providing that kind of family unity."

"Yes. Of course I am," Thane admitted. He noticed her fingers, long and slender, as they touched the rim of the cup. Tender and competent hands. "I believe I'm doing the best job of parenting I'm capable of doing, but it doesn't compensate for mother love, that kind of family unity you experienced with your parents."

When his gaze came to Meghan's, she shied from it. "Thane, this woman who would fit into the life-style you dream about; do you think she exists?"

"She exists," Thane said, his gaze on Meghan.

"Maybe only in your dreams, Thane."

"In that case, my sweet Meghan, I'll grow old alone," Thane said, looking back to the fire. His stomach was twisting in knots. She was the one who'd captured his mind, woven herself into the fabric of his dreams. She could offer the kind of love he needed to sustain him. But it would be only in his dreams.

When Thane realized he'd been hovering in thought, he cleared his throat, turned to smile at Meghan. "I'm ready for more cocoa. How about you?"

"I think I could handle another cup," Meghan said, returning his smile when he stood and reached for her cup. "Heavy on the marshmallows, please."

"Marshmallows are the only legitimate reason for drinking cocoa," he said.

"That's a fact," Meghan agreed. As she looked up at him, she became sad at the idea that he could grow old alone, at the knowledge that he excluded her from his dreams. And the most depressing thought of all was that he couldn't get past the disillusionment of his failed marriage.

Still, she smiled as she handed him her cup, because she clung to the idea that there had to be a way to make Thane open his mind to her.

"I'll stick the cocoa in the microwave," Thane said as he took the cup from Meghan and turned to go into the kitchen. "Won't take five minutes, and the marshmallows will be melted to a gooey state, just the way I like them."

"The gooier the better," Meghan said, leaning her head back on the sofa. "How about that, Thane? We—friends—have in common a liking for gooey marshmallows."

Thane looked over his shoulder to see Meghan's eyes had already closed. "Yeah. How about that. Gooey marshmallows make a solid foundation for a relationship."

Meghan bolted upright. "Maybe not solid...but sticky?" When Thane glanced over his shoulder, she nailed him with an accusing look.

"Relax, Meghan. I wasn't implying anything," Thane said. He pivoted in the doorway to confront her. "Our problem isn't a lack of having things in common. Our problem is a lack of time to discover all we have in common."

"We've packed a lot of living and learning about each other in a few short hours tonight, haven't we?" Meghan argued.

"Yes, indeed. We have. But there won't always be a blizzard on hand to keep us together—and keep the world at bay," Thane said, smiling but definitely not joking.

Meghan got the point. When he said "the world," he meant her work. "Oh—go fix the cocoa. Please," she sputtered.

Ten minutes later Thane returned to the front room, carrying two steaming cups of cocoa topped with marshmallows. As he expected, Meghan was sleeping.

She'd slid lengthwise, her head on a pillow. Her legs were bent at the knees, pulled up, and her hands were folded together between her knees. The exhaustion he'd seen in her face was gone, replaced with the peaceful expression that came with dreamless sleep.

He placed the cups on the end table, intending to cover her with the afghan from the back of the sofa. As inviting as he found her, he wouldn't touch her as he tucked the afghan in place. He wouldn't touch her because she needed a man who would give her room, not suffocate her with the kind of love he would have for her if he allowed himself to love her. It wasn't a question of falling in love with her. That he could do. It had become a battle of not allowing himself to love her, knowing that were she to love him in return he would make them both miserable.

He reached for the afghan. The reflection of the flames from the fire caused shadows under her eyes. Mesmerized by the arching contours, he bent closer and touched her cheek with his fingertips. In her sleep her lips formed a kiss. He brushed the smoothness of her lips with his fingertips, taking the kiss from her.

She didn't waken but murmured and smiled.

He got to his knees, moving his fingertips back over the gentle curve of her cheek, the tip of her nose, the delicate question mark of her ear, memorizing the feeling of her skin, her bone structure.

Her lashes fluttered open. "Cocoa ready?" she asked. Then, seeing through the haze of waking that Thane was sitting on his haunches, his hands on his knees, smiling at her, she stated, "I must talk in my sleep."

"You don't talk, but you sing when you snore," Thane said, caressing her with his voice, incapable of not demonstrating the tenderness he was feeling for her.

She half propped herself on her elbow, frowning. "I don't snore."

"Ah, but you do, sweet Meghan. 'Twas 'Finnigin' you were snoring."

"Finnigin your foot," Meghan responded softly. "Were you touching me, or was I dreaming?" He'd been touching her. She'd wakened with the feel of his fingertips on her lips, wanting him. Instantly, without preamble.

"A little touching is permissible between friends," Thane said languorously. He leaned forward, murmuring, "And a kiss is permissible."

Meghan lulled in the warmth of her desire and the desire she saw reflected in Thane's eyes. She was sluggish, but her senses were agonizingly alert. Never before had she felt her skin tingle in anticipation of a man's touch. Never had she been so tuned in to the soft sound of a man's whispered breathing, she was thinking as his lips closed in on hers.

Thane groaned. Her lips were sweet, yielding. Slowly, very slowly, he eased his lips from hers to take nibbling kisses across her chin, down her throat, following the deep V of her shirt so his last kiss came over her heart and he felt her heart fluttering.

He raised his head to meet her gaze. "From the moment I saw you, I've been fighting the need I have for you, sweet woman. And at first I called it infatuation." Half smiling, he ran his fingers along the length of her neck in a tactile adventure. No static electricity, this, he thought. What is it? Her spirit touching mine. "But now, knowing you, Meghan—it isn't a foolish attachment I feel, but something much more complicated."

Meghan extended her hand to caress his chin. She wove her fingers into his beard, knowing where they were going and that it would have to be her decision to stop. But there was no thought in her mind of stopping the enchantment of the moment.

"I've wondered how your beard would feel," she whispered hoarsely. "Now I know. Your beard is as soft as Finnigin's fur. And you are softer still. A very gentle man."

Thane turned his head to rest his cheek in her palm for a moment. "I don't want to hurt you, Meghan. Or be hurt," he said, then raised his gaze to study Meghan's face, and his self-doubts vanished. She understood how insecure he felt. Yet only trust and faith in him were reflected in her eyes.

She ran her thumb over his lips, whispering, "Sh, my sweet man, sh. Trust me." He groaned, gathered her into his arms, lifted her from the sofa to the floor and settled her on his lap.

Meghan molded her body to Thane's, resting her head against his shoulder. "This feels so right," she whispered. "So right."

There was a fever to their intimate caressing and the kisses they were sharing, but a sense, too, of going slowly as they learned about each other. What Meghan had known with their first kiss was confirmed over and over again. She'd been changed. She was independent by nature, but that independence was being tempered by her desire to share herself totally with Thane.

Lovingly, Thane adjusted Meghan in his arms and removed her cardigan. Paused to kiss her. When her shirt fol-

lowed the sweater, he kissed her again. He unsnapped her
bra, then eased her back into a cradling position in his arms
to take joy for a moment in the perfection he'd uncovered.

Meghan hadn't murmured a word of either protest or encouragement. Fascinated, she was watching the expression
on Thane's face. His eagerness made her eager. His pleasure brought her pleasure. And each time his lips came to
hers, her response was to feed at his lips hungrily, as if to
sate the ache deep within her body. As she lay sweltering
under the heat of his gaze she smiled, satisfied that he'd not
been disappointed in her.

"Ah, my sweet Meghan," Thane whispered thickly,
"you're beautiful."

With his words, Meghan felt her nipples harden, then
ripen when his fingertip grazed them. When he gently
cupped her breasts and bent his head to suckle at first one
and then the other, she moaned, "Thane. This isn't fair. It
isn't fair at all."

Thane's laugh was low. "We want to be fair, don't we?"
he said, releasing her long enough to slip off his sweater.

Before he'd managed to toss the sweater aside, Meghan
was running eager fingers through the golden mat of hair on
his chest. "And you, my sweet man, are also beautiful," she
said. The enchantment, the jubilation she was feeling
sounded in her voice. She ran her fingers up and over the
muscles of his shoulders, down the length of his arms, then
brought his arms around her.

When he tightened his embrace, it was warm, silky skin
on warm, silky skin before a stimulating tickling of hair on
her breasts caused Meghan to tremble. New sensation after
new sensation. She circled his neck with her arms. "You're
my captive," she said. "This is bliss."

Thane kissed her again, sucking the life's breath from her,
taking it for himself, slanting his lips, pressuring hers to
admit him to possess her. When her lips parted and the tip

of her tongue roamed the outline of his lips, he knew who'd submitted, who owned, who was giving. Who'd been possessed. He broke away, breathless.

"That is bliss, my sweet Meghan."

She leaned from him as far as he'd allow her. "I stand corrected," she said. "Your kiss is bliss—and Thane, there is something you should know. I've never been sweet-tempered. I only want to be sweet for you."

"I'll remember that...you're only sweet for me," Thane whispered, kissing her russet lashes closed, nuzzling the fine hair around her ear. "Feels like chick down."

It took a moment for Meghan to rouse from the spiraling orbit she was riding to say, "A chick, Thane? A chick?" She nipped his nipple with her teeth.

Shock waves were roaring through Thane's body, demanding to be released, but the sensual pleasure he was getting from holding, fondling her was too intense to relinquish immediately.

"I was trying to be romantic," he said. "I meant a newborn chick, of course. Unfeathered."

"A newborn chick is so much more romantic." Meghan smiled, nipped his shoulder with her teeth, his neck, under his chin, his earlobe.

"You're distracting me from further clarification," Thane said. "You are interested in what I have to say, aren't you?" He rotated her nipple between his fingers.

Meghan worked the tip of her tongue behind his ear until he groaned. "Of course I'm interested."

"A chick is deceptively sturdy," Thane said, his voice sounding dry. "Independent even before hatching, and after hatching it doesn't really need anyone in order to survive."

Meghan hugged Thane close. "That may be true of some chicks, but *this* chick is beginning to understand she needs the nourishment of your love to keep it alive."

"Ah, Meghan. I want to give you the nourishment of my love. But would my love always be enough? Is love ever enough?"

There was his reservation sounding again, Meghan realized. His fear. His lack of trust in her. It was as if the blizzard pounding on the door had won a victory, shoved the door open and a cold blast of air was sweeping in on her. She'd been deceiving herself. Lovemaking wasn't a prelude to solidifying a relationship between them. It wasn't a prelude to commitment, but a compromise to chemistry. She laid her hands on the chest that had already become so dear to her that withdrawing caused her heartache.

"Meghan?"

"You *want* to love me, but even with love you don't think there's a future for us, do you, Thane?"

"I want a future for us, Meghan. I do!" Any thought he had of tightening his hold on her, kissing her into submission, was discouraged by the snapping of her eyes.

"But you aren't convinced there will be, are you?"

"No. I'm not convinced."

Meghan slid from his lap and reached for her bra. She pivoted on her buttocks so her back was to him. "I want you to make love to me. But this is wrong for us," she said as she slid the straps into place.

"Nothing has ever been more right. Come back to me," he urged.

"Nothing has ever been more right for me, either," Meghan agreed. With the bra snapped, she turned back to face him. "But I won't risk having you see our lovemaking as having been born of chemistry and not of the mind. I don't want you to see lovemaking with me as entrapment. Or feel obligated to continue a relationship with me simply because we made love."

"I'm willing to take the chance if you are," Thane said, aching from her withdrawal from him.

Meghan ignored the entreaty in Thane's eyes, his open-palmed gesture. "I'm not willing to chance it, Thane. I think I'm falling in love with you. And the biggest mistake we could make would be to make love."

Thane half laughed as he ran his fingers through his hair. "Meghan, I think I'm going crazy. You're starting to make sense to me," he said wryly. He shook his head in bemusement. "We have slipped beyond friendship, casual love-making, into a serious consideration that what we are feeling is love. And you're right. Now, because we might be in love, it would be wrong to make love."

"What we need is time to really get to know each other," Meghan said.

"Haven't I been saying that?" Thane leaned back against the sofa, crossing his legs at the ankles. It was going to be a long night. Not of lovemaking, as he'd envisioned.

"I'm going to ignore the insinuation I heard in that remark, Thane. What I'm thinking is . . . maybe we should go steady," Meghan said.

"Now I've heard everything!" Thane laughed. "Do couples even go steady anymore?"

"I don't care what other couples do. I don't want you casting glances at other women until we've got this settled. And we can't be engaged, because that's a commitment and you aren't ready for a commitment." She eyed him meaningfully. "Because you're still using my career as a road-block."

"Boy!" Thane said drolly. "I do admire the logical way you're handling this."

"Don't get smart with me, MacDougal. And don't knock going steady until we've tried it."

"Frankly, I thought being friends was kind of fun."

Meghan grinned at him. "Going steady will be fun. Now, do you want to go steady or not?"

"Damn. I don't believe I'm allowing you to manipulate me into this."

"I went along with the friendship thing," she reminded him.

"Okay. We're going steady. Wait a minute—is this a platonic steady?" Thane asked.

"Naturally."

"It'll never work."

"Kissing is permissible. And lots of cuddling and...necking."

"Necking? Exactly what areas of the body are involved in necking?"

"From the neck up, I think. You know," she said, struggling to maintain a decent attitude, "that is an interesting question. Where's your dictionary? We'll look the definition up."

"We make our own rules."

"Neck up," Meghan said.

"Toes up."

Meghan feigned serious pondering. "Uh, shoulders up."

"Knees," Thane fired back.

"Waist."

"You've got it, sweet Meghan. I'm still in great need—of being close to you. Come to me."

Thane opened his arms and Meghan, without hesitation, slid into them.

Meghan woke to the sun streaming through the east window of the bedroom. For a moment she lay, smiling, knowing that she woke this day to see Thane, that it was in his home she'd slept, although not in his bed. She was in the spare bedroom. Still, her waking was not routine. She felt nothing was banal anymore, but fresh and momentous.

The sun *was* shining, she thought again, this time with the realization that the blizzard that had locked out the world was over. Soon, too soon, the world would force its way back in on them. She threw back the covers, bounced from the bed.

In ten minutes, dressed to go outside, she stepped from the house. She took a deep breath of the brisk air and raised her hand to shield her eyes from the sun, which was already softening the snow. She saw no sign of Thane, but she heard a tractor and followed the sound until she found him grinding feed by the corncrib.

"What can I do to help?" she asked as Thane moved from the grinder to meet her.

"How are you at washing down farrowing houses?"

Meghan faked a groan. She was out of her bean with delight at seeing him. Their night had been one glorious exploration of minds and bodies—within the limits of the rules of necking—and how long had it been since she'd last seen him? Four whole hours. "Got a power washer?"

"You bet," Thane said. He reached for Meghan. She slid into his arms, wrapped her arms around his neck. Even through the thickness of their layers of clothing his body thrummed from the contact.

Their kiss ended as quickly as it had started.

"Good morning, my sweet Meghan."

"Good morning, my sweet man."

Thane pawed at her chin with a gloved hand. "The way you look at me, the way your voice sounds calling me your sweet man, makes me feel as if I'm someone special."

"You are special. But keep it in mind that only I can make you feel special." She leaned back in his arms, gazing up at his features.

"Enough of talking about me," Thane said lightly. "You're quite beautiful in *my* green stocking hat." He pulled on the tasseled ball that sat on the crown of her head.

"I thought my ski mask would be a bit too much, fashionwise," she said, scrunching her nose. "You know a lady isn't wise to overdress. Makes her look tawdry."

"Oh, yes. Really tawdry."

"I'm so glad to see that you appreciate what I went through, dressing so I'd be attractive for you," Meghan said. She batted her lashes. "Notice: I set the cap on my head. Just so. At a cocky angle." She feigned primping, laughed, then planted a big kiss, deliberately loud, on his lips.

She started to leave his arms. Thane restrained her. "Where do you think you're going? I don't think I've finished kissing you yet."

"You're grinding, remember. I'm going to wash down the farrowing house."

"I was only teasing about you washing down the farrowing house. You don't have to do a thing but keep me company."

Meghan backed away. "I'm going to make myself useful. I may not know how to cook, but I do know about washing down farrowing houses. See you later," Meghan said. She took off, high-stepping through the snow toward the farrowing house.

Meghan tried to make herself one with the side of the nursery while she waited for Thane to reappear. A few minutes before, she'd seen Thane go inside the nursery. She was trying not to laugh. She was in ambush, holding a huge soft snowball, waiting for the moment his golden head appeared at the door. She had him! He would never expect this. He'd get the best of her in a snowball fight, but she'd get the first snowball thrown—

Her head snapped forward; loose snow flew by. Thane's laughter rang across the barnyard, and she spun and saw he was lumbering toward her from the back of the nursery.

"Did you think I wouldn't see you through the window? You should have checked for back doors before you tried to ambush me," he called.

Meghan let fly with her snowball, yelled with glee when she nailed him on the head. She grabbed more snow from the low roof of the nursery and turned to flee around the corner where the snow hadn't drifted.

His voice taunted her. "Come out, come out, wherever you are, my little chick!"

Meghan laughed, covering her lips with her glove to muffle the sound.

"You know you're going to have to pay for trying to ambush me, sweet Meghan."

The sensuous sound of his voice gave Meghan a thrill. Oh, yes, she knew she would pay. She was planning on it. But the game was most important now. Listening, she decided he was coming around the building to her right, so rather than creeping away, she advanced in that direction, knowing he'd never expect a frontal attack. She'd get him at the corner—

"Gotcha!" Thane said, wrapping his arms around her from the back. He slid his chin along her cheek on the softness of his silken beard.

Meghan turned her head to brush her lips in the hollow beneath his ear. The snow dropped from her hand.

"You do surrender sweetly," Thane murmured through the kiss. "I don't know if I can let you go, Meghan."

"Don't threaten me with release," Meghan said, her voice low.

Thane sighed. "I won't threaten you with release. But if you decide you want release, I'll do it without fighting you, because I care so much for you, my dear, sweet friend. My going-steady person."

"Kiss me. Just kiss me. Let's allow what will happen to happen," she was saying as his lips quieted her.

* * *

Two weeks later, it was far from quiet as Thane glanced around a table near the window of a truck stop. There were definitely more faces present than he and Meghan had planned on the night before when they'd talked about taking in the Angus cattle show and sale in Sioux Falls. They'd figured on an early start and breakfast along the way. He'd known he was going to have to share Meghan with Murphy today, but *this* he hadn't foreseen.

An apologetic Meghan had explained the presence of Chip and Nance: "What could I say, Thane? Chip showed up at my house for an early visit, and when he found me getting ready to leave for Sioux Falls, he hinted broadly that he liked cattle sales." And what could she have said when Chip had gone home to get ready and Nance came marching over to ask why she couldn't go along if Chip and Murphy were going? By the time Tina arrived to find out what her daughter was up to, Meghan had already told Nance she could go.

So it looked as though togetherness of the kind he'd been aching for since their last kiss after the movie in Sioux City the previous night was going to be impossible. And yet being with Meghan under any circumstances was better than not being with her.

When Meghan glanced up and caught Thane looking at her, his smile made her smile. They were separated by the table and their conversation was interrupted by the enthusiastic chatter of three young people, but Meghan felt happy, content, a feeling that hadn't left her in the past two weeks.

She formed the words, "Isn't going steady fun?" on her lips and chuckled when Thane mouthed back, "Oh, loads." It was enough, she reflected. Thane was near. His smile was for her alone, as it had been last night. What was the name of the movie they'd seen? She couldn't remember!

Maybe she would have remembered if Thane hadn't slipped his arm over her shoulder the minute they'd sat down in the back row of the theater. When the lights dimmed, he'd feathered his fingers over one ear while he kissed the lobe of the other. They had carried on shamelessly. Until last night she'd never necked in a theater in her life.

She glanced at Thane. He winked. Good grief! She was still feeling wickedly sexy. She felt a blush creeping up her neck. To distract herself, she looked around the diner. Truckers and family groups seemed to make up the majority of those eating.

She was pleased at the thought that Thane, the children and she must look like a family. She felt a little smug, too. He must be admitting to himself how good she was with children, and seeing that mothering came naturally to her.

"Well, hate to break up this little family gathering," Thane said, "but I think we'd better hit the road, or we'll get to the show too late to look around before the sale starts."

That mental telepathy is pretty strong stuff, Meghan thought, smiling down into Nance's cherub face. Black-eyed, black-haired, Nance *was* a little darling. Meghan couldn't believe any teacher, even joking, could say Nance had given her an ulcer.

"Better drink your milk, Nance. We're ready to go," she said.

"No," said the sweet little thing.

Chapter Eleven

Meghan was dumbfounded. The child never said no to her. "No?"

"No, please?" Nance asked with an angelic smile on her cherub face.

"Uh-oh. Here we go." This was from the sandy-haired, freckle-faced Chip, who, having slipped his baseball hat on in anticipation of leaving, slipped it off again, sighing. "We're going to be here forever and forever!"

"Of course we won't be here forever," Meghan said, confident of winning the battle of wills in which Nance had engaged her. "Nance wants to go to the cattle show, don't you, Nance? And so you'll drink your milk."

"No."

"No to drinking your milk or to the cattle show?" Meghan asked through pressed lips.

"No milk." Nance folded her arms across her chest and mimicked Meghan's pressed lips.

"Think how nice it will be to grow up big and strong," Meghan said.

"Nope."

"Nice try, Meghan," Thane said. "That one never worked on me, either, when Dad tried it."

Meghan flashed him a smile that held a trace of menace, then turned back to work on Nance. "If you drink your milk, you can have some popcorn at the sale," she said, thinking, My darling little Nance has a bullheaded streak wider than a skunk's stripe.

"That's bribery," Thane appraised.

Meghan eyed Thane. "I know what it is, thank you," she said.

"She don't like popcorn," Chip said.

"Try grape soda," Murphy offered helpfully.

"Grape soda," Meghan offered.

Nance gnawed on her lip, considering.

Murphy rapped his fingers on the table. Chip was kicking the leg of the table with his toe. Thane had fallen into a quiet observation of her that Meghan found totally unnerving. Was he thinking that she couldn't handle a four-year-old even though *that child* was showing every indication of growing up to be a hood?

"Nope," Nance announced. "Don't want grape soda, either."

"See?" Murphy said. "Nance and Mary Jane did give Mrs. Blair ulcers."

"Paddle her butt," Chip advised. "That's what Mom does."

Meghan glanced across the table. Thane was turning his fork over and over and over, while Chip leaned back in his chair and kicked the table leg. Murphy had come forward to the chin-in-the-hand pose while studying the situation.

"I couldn't spank Nance," Meghan said.

"Why not?" Thane asked calmly. "The way she's acting, she needs it."

"Uncle Thane!" Nance whimpered.

Meghan glared at Thane. "Now see what you've done!" Nance's whimper vanished. She smiled up at Meghan. Why, the little viper! Meghan thought. Four years old and she's playing both sides of the table!

"I knew it was a mistake to bring the *baby* along," Chip said.

Nance's mouth quivered again.

"She's not a baby," Meghan said. All they needed now was a crying child. "Please, Nance. Drink the milk."

"No!"

"Cockroaches!" Meghan snapped.

Nance wailed. "There's bugs in my milk!"

Every head in the café swiveled in unison to look in their direction. "No, no, no, there aren't cockroaches in your milk," Meghan whispered. She felt terrible. She picked up the glass, trying to show Nance that there were no cockroaches in the milk.

Nance leaned away from Meghan, covering her mouth with her hand as if protecting herself from an anticipated force feeding. "Cockroaches is bugs! I seen 'em on television," Nance wailed.

An ashen-faced middle-aged waitress rushed up, asking in a hushed voice, "Did you see a cockroach?"

Meghan looked across the table and silenced the giggling Murphy and Chip with a look. "There's been a little misunderstanding," she said, trying to sound calm. "I'm only trying to get this child to drink her milk."

The woman said, disgusted, "By telling the poor little thing her milk has *cockroaches* in it?" She wheeled away, muttering, "The things some mothers won't do."

"You feel like paddling her now?" Chip asked, still hopeful.

"Of course not," Meghan said. But she was getting there. "Nance. I say 'cockroaches' instead of saying a naughty word. There are no bugs in your milk."

"What naughty word, Auntie Meg?" Nance demanded.

"Never mind," Meghan said with resignation. She wasn't going to win with Nance. "Forget the milk. Let's get out of here."

Nance grinned.

"We're not forgetting the milk, Meghan," Thane said.

Meghan looked up and saw what she knew she'd see, a thoroughly disgruntled man. "You told Nance to drink her milk. Now, you've seen Nance drink milk and I've seen her drink not one but two and three glasses of milk at a sitting, so it isn't a question of not liking milk," he said to Meghan, then directed his attention to Nance. "Why don't you want to drink that milk, Nance?"

"It ain't chocolate," Nance said. "And Murphy got chocolate."

"It isn't chocolate," Thane agreed.

"I want chocolate."

"You should have ordered chocolate, but you didn't. That's the breaks of the game, Nance. Now, drink that glass of milk and remember to order chocolate milk the next time if you want it." When Nance appeared to be considering alternatives, Thane said firmly, "Now, Nance. I'll give you five minutes."

He looked at his watch, then leaned back in the chair and smiled at Nance. Nance smiled back, picked up the glass and began drinking. He sighed with relief. Nance could be as stubborn as her mother if she put her mind to it. He'd lucked out.

Meghan glanced at Murphy. She should have taken Murphy's warning to heart when he told her what had happened to poor Mrs. Blair. Her gaze drifted to Thane, who was frowning, and her spirits took a cold-bath plunge. Obviously he was thinking about how badly she'd handled Nance.

"Done," Nance announced as she shoved her chair back from the table. "We can go now."

Well, goody, goody gumdrops, Meghan thought as she watched Nance sail toward the door. Smiling brightly at Thane, she said, "It looks as if we're at least going to make it in time for the sale."

"He'll go for eighteen hundred at least," Thane said as they waited for the bull he and Meghan had picked out during the show to enter the sale ring.

The three children had gone to find grape soda, leaving Meghan and Thane alone, with the exception of the two hundred or so other bidders gathered in the bleachers for the sale. It was only that he *felt* alone with Meghan. Intimately alone.

"He's exactly what you wanted, Thane. A two-year-old, good bloodlines," Meghan said. "Maybe he'll go for less."

"Not the way the bidding has gone on the other bulls. And I really can't afford eighteen hundred. I've got seed corn and fertilizer to pay for yet."

The moment Meghan had seen the bull, Heritage Don, without saying anything to Thane and before he'd asked for her opinion, she'd decided to bid on it. In the arrangement she had with her father, she provided a bull every two years in return for running her cows on his range. That is, she had intended to bid until Thane had started talking about buying him. But maybe now they could work something out together.

"I propose a partnership in buying Heritage Don," Meghan said. "Fifty-fifty."

"Why would you want to buy a bull?" Thane said shortly. He hadn't intended to be short with Meghan, but she'd come up with that one out of the blue. Still, she probably had a reasonable explanation for the abruptness of her offer. It wasn't like her to be offering charity. "I'm sorry, Meghan. I shouldn't have snapped at you," he added quickly.

"An apology does not constitute an explanation, Thane, and I want an explanation for why you tried to bite my head off."

"I'd rather not explain."

"We're going *steady*, remember?" Meghan said, lowering her voice seductively. "We're trying to work things out between us."

"For a second, when you said partnership, I felt like a kept man, the way I used to feel when Ralph Palmer offered handouts."

"Cassandra's father?"

"Yes. Cassandra's father. Cassandra thought my job as a feed-control analyst wasn't the kind of position the husband of an up-and-coming lawyer should have. So Ralph created a partnership, a vice-presidency position for me. My job was to entertain clients when they were in the city." He paused, looking startled. "Do you know, I've never before told anyone about how I felt, not even Bill and Tina."

Dismay and anger flared in Meghan. No wonder Thane felt the way he did about her being a veterinarian. Cassandra had demeaned him, belittled his vocation, held her career and position up to him.

"I'm sorry Cassandra hurt you so badly, Thane." Meghan ran her fingers down the length of Thane's palm, then back up to his wrist. "I have the feeling you were vice-president material."

"Take my word for it. I'm a damn good chemist and a damn good farmer, but a corporate officer I wasn't." Thane tilted his head to get a better look at Meghan. No patronizing, no pity in her eyes.

"Okay, sweet woman. I've explained why I snapped at you. Now, please let me know why you'd like to go fifty-fifty on Heritage Don."

Meghan quickly told him about the arrangement she had with her father, then said, "You'll use the bull with your cows for two years and then I'll ship him to Kansas." She started to remove her hand now that they were talking business. Thane smiled and held on to it.

"Marriage is a partnership. Fifty-fifty. Is this like a marriage?" he asked.

"No matter what happens between us personally, Heritage Don is strictly business." Meghan wanted Thane to understand she wasn't trying to tie him into anything or make him beholden to her, the way Ralph Palmer had done.

"Fifty-fifty. Eighteen hundred tops?" Thane said by way of agreement.

"Two thousand?" Meghan saw nothing of the crowd around them, heard no voices other than Thane's.

"I can handle that." He leaned close, brushed her ear with his lips. "I dare you to kiss me to seal the bargain."

Meghan tried to look unflappable. "They're bringing Heritage Don into the ring." But she couldn't resist. She kissed him quickly, then looked straight ahead, pretending she hadn't done it.

"I haven't gotten my hands on you all day. I'm dying," Thane whispered. He raised her hand, kissed her knuckles.

His beard brushing her hand caused Meghan's breathing to become all fluttery. Her insides turned over. "Thane. Aren't you touching me right now?" He kissed her hand again. She couldn't stand the wild sensations. "Stop it. People are looking."

"They'll think I'm whispering strategy."

"To my knuckles?" Meghan's laugh was low, intimate.

Thane lowered her hand, put his lips to her ear. "Now they'll know I'm whispering strategy."

Meghan's entire body was quivering in delight. "The way I must be blushing, they'll know what kind of strategy you're whispering."

Thane spotted a dark-haired man showing too much interest in Meghan. He possessively slipped his arm around her waist. When the man glanced in her direction again, Thane quirked a brow. The man returned the gesture as if saying, Okay, buddy. Got the message.

He handed his bidding card to Meghan. "You do the bidding."

"Why me?"

"I want to watch you in action. Look at you."

Meghan didn't remind him that for the past five minutes he had been looking at her—very intently. She snuggled his fingers to her. Ever since she and Thane had climbed into the bleachers, a blond, blue-eyed woman in the first row had had her eye on Thane, trying to get his attention. And she was at it again.

Meghan leaned into Thane's arms, and when the blonde's gaze finally came to Meghan, Meghan smiled sweetly as if to say Look somewhere else, darlin'. The blonde's eyes went vacant-looking before she turned away. Meghan loved it, the feeling of Thane's belonging to her and the feeling of her belonging to Thane.

Thane began playing *rat-a-tat-tat* on Meghan's waist with his fingers. The beat pulsated through her body. "Thane, I need to concentrate."

"Concentrate away," Thane said.

"Dammit. I can't concentrate with you doing that!"

"Doing what?" Thane asked innocently.

"Just stop it," Meghan said as the auctioneer announced, "Ladies and gents. Now in the arena, Bull 876, Heritage Don, out of Noble Donna and Jim Don."

Thane squeezed Meghan's waist, and she obliged him by jumping. The auctioneer cried, "We start the bidding at one thousand. Do I hear it?"

Three ring men scanned the bleachers for bidders.

A card flashed. "Thousand right here," a ring man yelled, and the bidding was off and running.

Meghan craned her neck this way and that to get a better view of the competition. A young farmer, clean-cut and intent, had bid the thousand. An older man sitting in a lawn chair at ringside came in fast at one thousand one hundred. She loved a cattle auction, the spirit of bidding—the finessing, the psychology, the pace.

"They're up to fourteen hundred, Meghan," Thane said out of the side of his mouth. "If you're going to get a bid in, you'd better do it before it gets out of our range."

"I know what I'm doing," Meghan said, her lips barely moving. "The time to get in isn't now."

The young farmer held the bid at fifteen hundred. The older man slid his feed cap back, rubbed his bald head and offered fifty dollars more.

To Meghan's left she saw the real competition, a middle-aged man wearing cowboy boots, hat and jeans and leaning against the gate leading to the ring. Looking bored, he flicked his bidder number and took the bid at one thousand six hundred and fifty. The young farmer dropped out.

"It's getting into rich man's territory," Thane commented, grinning. Meghan's eyes were like an eagle's as she evaluated the other bidders. Her fingers on the bidding card were tense. Everything she did she did with spirit, throwing herself into it.

And talk about throwing herself into it, he thought, sweating as he recalled her impassioned response to him last night. He'd barely been able to walk out of the theater. She was being totally unrealistic if she thought they could limit themselves to kissing, fondling.... He moved his hand higher on her body.

When Meghan felt the warmth of Thane's hand close to her breast, she gave him a warning look.

He leaned close and whispered, "I loved the way your tongue and mine made love last night."

Meghan gasped. *That's* why she couldn't remember the name of the movie! In her distraction now, she flicked her hand and inadvertently entered the bidding when one ring man picked up the waggle of her card.

"Seventeen hundred," the ring man called, gesturing up to Meghan. "Right here!"

"Dammit, Thane," she said. "I didn't want in on the bidding right now."

"Well, my sweet Meghan, what can I tell you? You've got to learn to control your emotions."

"Are you serious about wanting Heritage Don?" she asked.

"Of course."

"Then stuff it—until later."

The cowboy looked up into the stands, met Meghan's gaze and narrowed his eyes. He said something to the ring man closest to him. "Yes. Yes. Yes!" the ring man bellowed.

"Eighteen hundred," the auctioneer said, then started his cry. Meghan propped her elbow on her knee, then very casually waggled it with two fingers. "Two thousand," her ring man called, and the auctioneer sang, "Got a two-thousand-dollar bid from the lady. Now a two thousand fifty. Two thousand—give me fifty."

Thane paled. "Good grief, Meghan. You gave him our best, and that cowboy isn't going to give up."

"He's bailing out," Meghan said complacently.

"What makes you think so?"

"Saw it in his eyes when he looked at me. Now, as I see it our only competition is the old guy in the lawn chair, the one who bid earlier. The more he sees of Heritage Don, the better he likes him. Look at him—he's debating right now whether or not to get back in. And he's looking at me to see if he can guess how far he'd have to go to outrun me."

The auctioneer paused in his cry. "Good-looking bull we got here, cowboy. Now, you going to keep bidding or stand there pawing the dirt?" he said, and resumed his cry while the audience laughed.

The ring man looked at the cowboy. The cowboy shook off. The ring man looked at the lawn-chair sitter, who looked up at Meghan and found her with her lips pursed, her eyes narrowed and her gaze unyielding. He shook off.

"I'll be damned, Meghan. You were right! We've got him!" Thane said, and gave Meghan a fast kiss.

For a moment Meghan forgot the ring action.

"Sold! Who's the buyer?"

"Forester-MacDougal," Thane called.

Meghan was in a semi-trance. Some kiss! In public, yet, broad daylight, and it was *still* some kind of awesome kiss.

"Sold to Forester-MacDougal. Couple holding card— raise the card, if you please." Meghan did, slowly. "Number one zero five. Congratulations. You got yourself one outstanding herd sire. Next up—"

"Let's go load our bull," Meghan said.

"I hate to see the day come to an end."

"End?" Meghan questioned. "We have the ride home ahead of us."

"Not long enough."

"Tell you what. I can be enticed to drive out for supper." She'd become a frequent evening guest at the Mac-Dougals', yet she knew what Thane meant. No matter how often or how long they were together, it wasn't often enough or long enough. Time stood still when they were apart, flew when they were together.

"It sounds as if the only thing you're interested in is my cooking," Thane said, feigning personal insult.

"I am interested in your cooking—among other things, which if mentioned in public would cause you considerable embarrassment."

"I doubt that," Thane said, laughing. "However, I'm momentarily appeased if you'll consider mentioning them later, in private."

"Oh, plan on it."

"Then you may come for supper. But for heaven's sake, don't let Nance manipulate you into bringing her along."

He laughed, but Meghan was sharply reminded about her inept handling of Nance. "I couldn't spank her, Thane. Maybe spanking was the answer, but she's not my child to spank."

"Actually, I don't believe in spanking children, either. I didn't know what my next move with Nance would have been if bluffing hadn't worked," Thane admitted.

"You were bluffing?"

"I was," Thane said.

"Well, you could have fooled me. But thank you for telling me. I was feeling pretty stupid about the whole affair, and especially sheepish because I'd been thinking you had to see how good I was with kids."

"You're terrific with kids," Thane said firmly.

Thane had done chores and checked on Heritage Don, who had settled down quickly in his new environment. Thane entered the kitchen to find Murphy on the telephone.

"Here's Dad now," Murphy said, handing the phone to Thane. "It's Doc. I'm going with her tomorrow after school to vaccinate some cows, if it's okay with you. Right now I'm going to check on Butternut and her calf,'' he said, and flew from the kitchen.

"Hello, Meghan,'' Thane said. She should have been on her way out here for supper. Since she wasn't, he knew before she spoke that she wasn't coming. "So Murphy's going to get a lesson in giving vaccinations tomorrow?''

"If it's okay with you.''

"Fine with me.''

"Thane, I hope I caught you before you started supper.''

"You aren't coming,'' Thane said.

"There were two calls on my answering service.''

"I understand,'' Thane said.

"Thane, I want to be with you.''

"Sure.'' Thane picked a pencil up from the desk, rolled it between his fingers.

"You're upset with me. I hear it in your voice.''

"I'm not upset, Meghan. Only disappointed.''

"I could try to stop by later,'' Meghan offered.

"You need to take care of yourself, Meghan. We had a long day. And a long night last night,'' he said, his voice low. "Pack it in when you get home and dream of me.''

"There hasn't been a night since I first saw you that I haven't.''

"Maybe you can stay for supper tomorrow night after you and Murphy get done with those cows,'' Thane suggested.

"I was hoping you'd ask. Love to. Have to rush now. Goodbye, my sweet man.''

She hung up. Thane tossed the pencil back to the desk and returned the receiver to the cradle. He missed her already. He reached for the phone to call her and tell her. He stopped himself. She was likely on the way out the door.

They'd been steadies for a month when early one morning, as Thane was harrowing with a disk, he spotted Meghan parking her pickup on the gravel road. When she climbed out, crawled through the fence and started walking across the field toward him, he shut off the tractor, climbed down, then leaned against the tire, waiting.

The early-morning sun threw flames from Meghan's hair. His breath caught. His body throbbed. He knew well the pattern of the sensual effect she had on him, always immediate, always intense and growing more urgent.

"Hello, stranger," he said as he lifted his cap and ran his fingers through his hair.

Meghan laughed. "Stranger? If it wasn't me you said good-night to last night around eleven, who was it?"

Thane took his handkerchief from his pocket and wiped the dirt from his forehead. Even with the cab, harrowing was a dirty job. "Oh, yes. I do remember you now. You're the one I cornered in the mudroom for a quick kiss goodbye because Murphy was lurking around the corner and you didn't want him to catch us.... You are that one, aren't you?"

"You're picking on me because I beat you at Monopoly. And Murphy beat you, too. Why don't you kiss me now? We're alone—no Murphy lurking in the bushes."

"I can't kiss you. I'm filthy."

Meghan took Thane's handkerchief from his hands and moved enticingly close. "I'll wipe a spot," she murmured, and proceeded to blot his lips, feigning concentration.

"You're killing me," Thane said, drawing her into his arms in spite of the dust on his clothes. When he kissed her he held her as if he were afraid she'd try to run away. "Kissing you is as refreshing as a cold glass of lemonade," he whispered against her cheek after the kiss.

Meghan was gasping when he released her. "First a chick and now lemonade?"

"Just can't keep the romantic side of my nature in check when you're around," Thane said, laughing. "Frankly, I thought it was apropos."

"Well, don't let it go to your head, but I've never had a compliment that pleased me more. You don't fool me anymore, Thane MacDougal. You are the most romantic man I've ever known...with the possible exception of my father." She linked her arm through his, and together they leaned against the tractor tire.

Thane chuckled. "Glad to know I'm in good company. Where are you on your way to?"

"Why couldn't I have been on my way here?"

"I know you, Meghan. You stopped here on your way to somewhere else," Thane said. The muscles in his chest were constricting. He knew she squeezed time out of her day for him. He was trying to accept that fact, trying to find some way to live with it, because he loved her.

He did love her and had for some time, but he'd been unwilling to admit it. Now that he had, he felt it with an intensity that frightened him and would frighten her if she knew, because with the admission, his resentment of her other love grew.

Thane knew she'd stopped for a few brief moments on her way somewhere else. They could be playing Monopoly or in the middle of eating dinner, and if someone called needing her help, she would pack up and go. Maybe not at the moment she hung up. But she would leave him to go.

He knew he was being unreasonable. Selfish. But he couldn't help how he felt. So what did he do with the knowledge that he loved her? Tell her? No, he kept it to himself and waited it out without knowing why he waited or what he expected to happen.

Meghan watched the tension develop in Thane's face, knowing he was thinking they spent too little time together. She came on the run to him at every opportunity, because she ached to be with him. Yet at each parting she felt guilty. It wasn't anything he said; it was how he looked at her, as he was looking at her now. As if a ponderous unhappiness were compressed behind his almond eyes. An unhappiness she couldn't penetrate.

Was she too much like Cassandra after all? Would Thane be happier with a woman who could devote all her energy and time to him? Maybe it was that kind of woman who could take away the unhappiness she saw in his eyes... his look of discontent.

The mere thought that she might not be the right woman for him sickened her. She molded herself to him now, attempting to deaden her doubts, convey to him how much she'd come to love him.

"I'm on my way to the Fergson place," she said at last. "A couple of their dairy cows are sick. I'll try to stop by sometime this evening." She had her lips pressed to his neck, so her voice was muffled.

"Try hard. I'll miss you until then. Kiss me quick, my sweet Meghan, then be gone," Thane said. Trying for the lightness he wanted to feel but couldn't, he eased her from his arms.

Later that night, Meghan rapped lightly at the Mac-Dougals' back door, then looked through the window. Thane came into view from the front room through the kitchen, yawning and slipping into a blue plaid shirt. When he opened the door, she stepped into his arms.

It had been a troubling day, and she was suffering pangs of self-doubt about her veterinary skills. She was in desperate need of his soothing administrations, the tranquillity she felt when she was with him.

"I shouldn't have stopped by so late. But I saw the light on in the front room," she murmured. As she leaned against him, the numbing weariness she'd been feeling began to ebb. "I needed to see you."

Thane massaged her back, her neck. "Every muscle is tied in knots. What's wrong?"

"I'm tired."

"It's more than tired. I talked to Tina earlier. She said you never came back to the clinic from the Fergsons' and she couldn't get you on the radio."

Meghan didn't have the energy to lift her head from Thane's chest. "Sixteen cows of Fergson's forty-cow herd are sick. Muscles of the tongue and throat paralyzed. One moment I'm sure it's botulism; the next, I don't know. I've never seen anything quite like it. If it is botulism . . . I think the problem has to be either with the silage or the feed. But Fergson's silage looks properly stored and the cows are well fed, no carrion lying around for them to chew on. . . . Still, I keep coming back to botulism. But I don't know."

Thane had never heard Meghan express vulnerability. "So what steps have you taken to this point?" he asked as he kneaded the muscles over her shoulder blades.

"That feels so good." She looked up and smiled fleetingly. "Two cows were showing signs of respiratory failure. I went on the assumption that I hadn't overlooked the diagnosis of an infectious disease, administered antitoxin and advised Fergson to stop using the feed and silage he'd had the cows on, until we knew for sure what was going on."

"Sounds like proper procedure to me," Thane observed.

"It's proper procedure if the problem is botulism. I sent samples of both the grain mixture and the silage to the state lab. They should be calling me with a report in a couple of days. But I dread thinking how many cows might be involved before the report comes back. And what if I'm wrong and it isn't botulism? I told Fergson I was giving him my best guess, but that's what it was—a guess. I told him I wouldn't be upset if he called in another vet for a second opinion."

"What did he say to that?"

Meghan sighed. "He's sticking with me."

"Wise man. You're the best," Thane said, smiling. "If you think it's botulism, then it's botulism."

"Thane, my sweet man. I needed you to tell me that, to bolster my flagging professional ego," she said. "But I'm wondering if I shouldn't ask one of the state vets to come out."

"If that needs to be done, you can do it tomorrow morning after I've analyzed Fergson's feed and silage. I should have that done by nine or nine-thirty."

"You? But you don't have the equipment, do you?"

"I don't," he said. "But I'll grab a sample of the feed and silage Fergson has been using and run it to the Newbrook Feed Processors in Sioux City. Hal Newbrook is a college buddy. He'll be more than happy to let me use their lab."

"I don't know what to say, other than thank you."

"You don't even have to say thank you. I'm happy knowing there's something I can do for you. Now, promise me you'll go home and not toss and turn all night worrying," Thane urged. He flicked his finger over her lips gently.

He was happy doing something for her! Meghan thought. He was the one always doing something for her, always giving. He gave one hundred percent of the time, while she took. His strength, his support, his nurturing of her body and soul, she took from him. And what did she give him in return? Only her love and desire for him. Even now, fighting fatigue, she wanted him.

"I can promise to go home and go to bed, even to sleep, but I can't promise I won't toss and turn all night long," she said.

"I'll have the workup for you no later than nine-thirty. I promise."

"Thane, sometimes you can be so dense. I wasn't talking about any feed analysis. I was talking about this insatiable desire I have to cuddle."

She pushed her body close to his, took his hands and secured them around her back, then shoved her arms under his arms and squeezed him to her almost desperately. "Thane, I love you."

Thane returned the gesture with the same air of desperation. "Oh, Meghan. And how I love you."

For long minutes they stood holding each other, and holding on to each other, as if neither was yet prepared to let go. It was as if both knew the love they had just declared, a love that should have been bringing them closer, was the very thing that was slowly but irrevocably driving them apart.

"Go home, my sweet Meghan," Thane said, though he wanted to carry her to his bed and wrap her in his arms while she slept, shield her from any nightmares.

"All right, my sweet man. I'll go home, unless you have something else in mind." What she wanted with every fiber of her being was for him to secure her in his arms forever, to tell her their love secured their future together.

"Go. It'll be morning before you get home." Thane avoided answering the question Meghan had asked indirectly. He could be her shield, her support, but he couldn't lie to her and assure her they had a future together. Nor would he offer her hope when he didn't feel it himself. He hated himself for his indecisiveness, but he loved her too much to tie her to him when his insecurity might end up making both of them miserable.

Meghan turned, stopped and wheeled in her tracks. "You didn't kiss me."

Smiling, Thane opened his arms. "I thought you were too tired to notice," he said as she ran back to him.

"Thane," Meghan said in lament. "I love you so much."

"I know, Meghan. I know," he said, seeking her lips.

Chapter Twelve

Thane walked into the clinic at ten with the printouts of the silage and feed analysis. Meghan rose from the chair behind the desk and came around to meet him.

"Hello, friend," Meghan said. "Tina's not here."

Thane grinned, opening his arms. Meghan stepped to him and kissed him long and hard before backing away to lean on the desk.

Thane took a deep breath. "Dynamite kisses from a dynamite lady. Ready to do business?"

Meghan nodded.

"You were right. Botulism. It's the silage."

Meghan took the paper and glanced over it, shaking her head. "I'd better get to the Fergsons' right away. I hope the dose of toxin the cows got is small." She looked up at Thane. "I owe you."

Thane grinned. "I'll think of a way you can pay me. But later. You're off to the Fergsons' and I'm off to start planting corn. See you—when?"

"Why don't you and Murphy come to my place for a late supper? Say, eight? Beef roast with trimmings."

"My love, the menu sounds delightful, but once I get into the field, I like to plant—"

"I know." Meghan laughed, thrilled with how naturally he'd called her his love. "You'll plant until dark. Now tell me who doesn't have time for whom?"

The question registered with Thane, though he didn't comment. He *was* telling her that his work in this particular instance came before she did, but of course while he planted he would be thinking of her....

He slipped his arm around her waist. "We'll be at your place for roast no later than nine. Walk me to the door?"

There they exchanged a quick kiss. Meghan stood watching as Thane climbed into Blythe, backed up, then headed down the street. She would see him at nine o'clock tonight. All they would manage again today would be an hour or two.

Each time this happened to them she questioned whether she was justified in thinking she could be wife, mother and veterinarian. And if she was questioning it, she thought, Thane must be wondering if he hadn't been right from the beginning.

But he simply had to understand that it was through her work that she found satisfaction. Through him she found happiness.

There it was again, she thought. She *took* happiness from Thane. In return she *gave* discontent....

She would not be there for him as a helpmate today. She would be at the Fergson place, not taking a mid-afternoon lunch to where he was working in the field. She wouldn't be available to run into town to the implement dealer to pick up some part he needed for a minor repair. And at noon he'd have to stop planting to check the farrowing house, because Murphy was in school and she wasn't there to do it.

She sighed heavily. Once, love had seemed so uncomplicated. The feeling itself was still uncomplicated. She loved
Thane. No question. But while she was a farm woman, was
she the right woman to be a farmer's wife? That was where
it got sticky. And Thane had known it would.

The concert had started at seven-thirty. Meghan, glancing at her watch, rushed up the sidewalk. It was only a
quarter to eight, and Tina had told her the kids tradition-
ally performed in the program in order from kindergarten
to high school. So she assured herself that she was in time
for Murphy and Charlene Kant's duet.

Over the past three weeks Murphy had reminded Meghan
several times about the concert. And each time, she'd
promised that she'd be there for the opening curtain. And
she *would* have been on time, too, if she hadn't had to clean
up first, she thought as she opened the schoolhouse door.
But she'd had to shower, wash her hair. She'd spent an hour
in the Smids' farrowing house.

Meghan smiled at the young girl who handed her a program, then opened the auditorium door. She stepped
through, waited for her eyes to adjust to the dim lighting,
then looked for a seat.

She sighed in relief. There was one at her right hand, back
row, on the aisle. She wouldn't have to announce her late
arrival by prancing around, looking for a seat. As she sank
onto the soft cushion, her gaze went around the auditorium. She smiled when she spotted Thane. That hair—no
one could miss it. It appeared he'd saved a seat for her.
She'd move up to sit by him when there was a break.

She glanced at her program. The third-grade students
were singing one of her favorite rounds. She'd made it in
time, she was thinking as she looked for Murphy's name
farther down on the program, grade five. After the third
grade came the seventh! Then the high-school chorus?

Hurriedly she scanned to the bottom of the lineup, back to the top. No! She hadn't made it in time! Murphy and Charlene had opened the concert.

Tears stung her eyes. She'd broken her promise to Murphy. Yet when Smid called, she'd tried to do it all—take care of her business and still make time for Murphy.

Because she loved Thane and needed him, she'd forced her way into his life with a total disregard for his fears and apprehensions, knowing but unwilling to admit the selfishness of her actions. She'd been single-minded, driven to prove Thane wrong. To prove that she could be all things to him.

Her shoulders slumped. Once, she'd believed she loved Thane too much to let him go; now she realized an unselfish love. A love so consuming she knew she had to release him. She couldn't be happy knowing the price of her happiness was the sacrifice of his dreams, his peace of mind....

After the concert Meghan moved outside with the crowd to wait for Thane and Murphy. She stood at the end of the sidewalk and to the side, saying hello to the concertgoers as they walked by her. Her heart did its usual racing when Thane strode into view.

"I'm glad to see you made it," he said. "When the seat next to me stayed empty I thought I'd been stood up."

Meghan forced herself to smile. He was wearing a navy knit shirt and casual pants and looked wonderful. And he was smiling at her, but behind the smile was that look again, as if his mind were in constant turmoil. She couldn't add further to his unhappiness. She was determined to make the break in an upbeat manner. No hysterics, no tears. If she wept, Thane, in his compassion for her, would take her into his arms. That couldn't happen. Her selfishness had to end.

"You look very handsome tonight, Mr. MacDougal," she said.

"I have to say that emerald-green number you're wearing turns me on," Thane said, slipping his arm around her waist.

"Hey, Doc," Murphy called as he and Chip approached. "Did you get here in time to hear my duet with Charlene?"

Meghan moved away from Thane. "No. I didn't." She couldn't look at Thane, because she couldn't stand to see his disappointment in her. "I'm sorry. There's no excuse for my breaking my promise to you." She fought to stop the trembling of her lips. Dammit. If she cried she'd hate herself.

Murphy grabbed her hand. "Gosh, Doc. Are you feeling bad?"

What is it about these MacDougal men? she wondered. Always touching me, making me feel better about myself when I shouldn't be. She smiled down into Murphy's face. "Sorry for myself is all, Murphy. I did want to hear you sing."

"There'll be plenty of times you can hear me sing. Tina told us that you had to go take care of one of the Smids' sows. I know you were thinking about me. So it's okay you missed it."

It wasn't okay, Meghan thought. But she squeezed Murphy's hand, straightened his hair, while Chip said, "I'll tell you one thing, Meghan. Chip and old Charlene really flubbed up!"

"Yeah," Murphy said, "we did."

"It wasn't that bad," Thane offered.

"Come on, Dad. It was bad," Murphy said.

"What happened?" Meghan asked.

Chip looked at Murphy. Murphy looked at Chip. They started giggling.

"That," Thane said, "is what happened. Chip was sitting in the front row. Murphy looked at him and giggled. Then Charlene giggled. Then everyone giggled and the music teacher stopped playing and started over."

"Told you it was pretty bad," Murphy said.

Meghan was smiling in spite of herself.

"Bad?" Chip said. "You stank, man." When Murphy pretended to lunge for Chip, they took off down the street, Murphy calling over his shoulder, "We going to the Greers' for a snack, Dad?"

"If Meghan isn't too tired," Thane replied.

"By the time I catch Chip to beat up on him, we'll be at his place. Okay?" Murphy yelled.

"Okay." Laughing, Thane turned to Meghan. "Mock war. Did you walk or drive over?"

"I ran, actually." Meghan could no longer pretend she was watching Chip and Murphy wind their way through the crowd. She met Thane's gaze. Whatever he was thinking, he'd concealed it behind an almond curtain. "I ran, but I still didn't get here in time."

Thane nodded. "I have Blythe parked at the end of the block."

As they started walking, Thane tried to slip his arm over Meghan's shoulder. "Please don't do that," she said. "I have something to say and I want to say it in a reasonable, unemotional manner. I can't when you're touching me." She stepped up her pace.

Thane noted the deep shadows under her eyes, but it wasn't weariness he heard in her voice. It was more like the sound of desperation. "Darned if this doesn't sound serious," he teased, matching her stride for stride. "Are we moving on from being steadies to something else?"

"It is serious, Thane. Don't try to tease me out of saying what I've got to say." She walked faster.

"I see that now. Air it," Thane said.

"From the beginning you questioned whether I could be a wife, mother and veterinarian, and I confidently insisted I could. But I've had to face the fact that you were right to question me, Thane. Being a wife and homemaker is a full-time career. I was wrong—"

"Meghan—"

Meghan kept her eyes averted. "Don't argue. Don't be compassionate because you love me. Just listen. You'd lived through the experience of being married to a woman whose career caused the marriage to fail. You'd been hurt, and badly. I remember telling you that love would be enough."

She stopped suddenly and wheeled to face him. "But loving each other isn't enough, because my work does make it virtually impossible for us to have the kind of life-style you missed having as a child and dream of having for Murphy. I simply cannot be a full-time wife and mother. So I'm calling it off, Thane. I want out of going steady."

Thane reached for her, trying to draw her into his arms. In desperation she ran from him, calling back, "Make an excuse for me to the Greers—anything. Tell them I had an emergency call."

"Stop where you are, Meghan," Thane yelled. "Dammit! You owe me an explanation. Let's get this settled tonight."

"I don't want to talk about it anymore. It's settled, dammit. It's settled." Meghan ran until she reached her house. Ran until she'd closed the door behind her, locked it against Thane and collapsed on the bed in a torrent of tears.

Meghan had been thinking about Murphy all day, because it was his birthday. But the sun was close to setting before she drove down the MacDougals' lane and stopped in the drive between the house and the barn. When she saw Murphy come from the barn, she opened the door of the pickup, climbed out, then turned to lift her companion from the seat.

"Oh, man! Oh, wow," Murphy squealed as he raced to take the Boston terrier pup from her arms. He nearly toppled backward under the weight of the wiggling animal.

Meghan grasped his shoulders and held him steady. "Happy birthday, Murphy."

"Gee, thanks, Doc. Wait until Finnigin sees him."

"You'll have to watch those two for a while to make sure the pup doesn't roughhouse and hurt Finnigin," Meghan cautioned.

"I'll watch, but I think they'll get along all right," Murphy said. "Man. He's a wriggly little devil." Murphy set the pup on the ground and dropped to his knees beside him, grasping the pup's head in his hands.

Meghan, grinning, ruffled Murphy's hair. "I've got a sack of puppy food in the back of the pickup," she said, turning to get it.

Murphy looked up. "I'll get the sack out, Doc. If you came while Dad was on the west forty checking for root worms, I was supposed to tell you that he wanted to talk to you."

Murphy was smiling. The pup was licking his cheek. And Meghan was being ripped apart. "Murphy, I think you made that up. Your dad didn't know I was coming this evening."

"No, I *didn't* make it up. Dad told me to tell you to find him, and I'm not supposed to tag along, because you guys had something to settle. Something about whether you were still friends. Anyway, he told me to stay out of the way."

Meghan gnawed at her lip. Murphy couldn't have dreamed that line up. Were they still friends? Did Thane want to keep the thing going when nothing could come of it but more hurting? And she was hurting. Since she'd last seen Thane, food had tasted like cardboard. She'd spent nearly the whole weekend holed up in the house, praying that all the livestock in the country stayed healthy, because she hadn't felt like facing anyone. It had even taken an hour of stern talking to herself before she'd gotten up the courage to drive out to deliver the pup.

"How did your dad know I'd be here today? I haven't, uh, talked to him recently."

The pup lapped Murphy's cheek with a wet tongue again. Murphy giggled. "Gosh, Doc. It's my birthday. We knew you wouldn't forget my birthday and that you'd come when you could.... You and Dad are fighting, aren't you?" Murphy stood, his eyes on Meghan, filled with concern.

"No. We're not fighting, Murphy."

"That's what Dad said. But you haven't called for nearly three whole days and you haven't been out for nearly three whole days, and it looks like fighting to me."

"Oh, Murphy. It isn't fighting," Meghan said. "I don't know what I'd call it, but it isn't fighting." She'd been wrong to run from Thane without giving him the chance to express his feelings. Apparently it wasn't settled in his mind. Maybe he wanted to chew her out. Well, as pushy as she'd been, she had a chewing-out coming.

"Doc," Murphy was saying shyly. "I really missed you. It just isn't fun without you around."

"Murphy," Meghan said, her voice catching, "I love you."

Murphy blushed, looked down, toed the ground with his tennis shoe. "I love you, too, Doc."

Meghan stepped to Murphy, drew him into her arms, held him. "Never forget I love you, Murphy. And whether your father and I can be friends or not, you and I will still have our special times together. That's a promise I'll keep."

She squeezed Murphy quickly, released him. "I'll see you later, Murphy. I'm going to look for your father."

"Boy, am I glad you're going, 'cause Dad said that if you wouldn't, I was to hog-tie you and sit on you until he got back, and I didn't know how I was going to do it." He grinned.

Laughing, Meghan turned away.

Thane stood up as Meghan climbed the hill toward him, her body casting a long, rippling shadow on the knee-high corn. He was aching to go to her, aching to have her in his arms, but he waited, wiping his hands on a handkerchief.

She came to within five feet of him, stopped and regarded him warily rather than rushing into his arms to smother him with kisses, as he'd hoped she would. His heart sank to his toes at what he'd done to this beautiful, loving and self-assured woman.

"I've never seen your eyes so lifeless, Meghan. Is it your personal life and not your professional life that's causing you problems?"

"That hit the nail on the head," Meghan countered. "What accounts for those dark half-moons under your eyes?" she asked. He looked so weary, so wretched. And she was the cause of it. She averted her gaze, looked at the sunset, at the ground.

"I've been losing sleep wondering whether or not I *have* a personal life," Thane said, stuffing the handkerchief into his pocket. "Now that we've established we're both miserable, shall we walk while we talk, Meghan, or alternately stare at the ground and the sunset instead of looking at each other?"

Meghan looked at him, narrowing her eyes. He wasn't going to be sweet or understanding. He was going to demand answers, and she wasn't sure she had any. "We walk," she said.

She set a slow pace, walking uphill again. Thane was in one row, she in another. There was less than three feet between them, but the distance seemed greater.

Thane took a deep breath, then took the plunge. "Can you tell me what caused you to decide you'd had enough of going steady?"

"Of course I can," Meghan said briskly. Those darn tears were threatening again. "When I was late getting to the concert, I took a seat in the back row. I looked around, saw the empty seat beside you and knew you'd saved it for me."

She stared down at the loamy soil, saw a small button-leaf weed, stopped, bent and pulled it. She glanced at Thane as she straightened. He'd also pulled a weed and dropped it in the row. When his gaze met hers, they exchanged tender smiles.

Meghan walked ahead slowly. "I knew that if I were the kind of woman you'd dreamed of sharing your life with, I would have walked with you into the auditorium. I would have been at your side."

She saw another button leaf and pulled it without missing a step. "Because I needed you, Thane, I was being selfish, riding roughshod over your feelings. You gave. I took. And marriage is a fifty-fifty proposition."

The tears in her eyes blurred the emerald color of the corn leaves, so they appeared to be swimming in an ocean. She shrugged, feeling helpless. "I can't contribute my share of the investment in marriage. That's it. That says it."

"Meghan," Thane began. His voice wavered. She'd moved ahead. She was wearing a lovely russet-colored blouse, not as lovely in color as her hair. "I once believed marriage was a fifty-fifty proposition, but I've realized it isn't. Loving can't be done in a calculating manner, or it isn't love."

He quickened his pace and came abreast of her. Meghan glanced at him, then looked away. They'd reached the hill's summit.

"You were right, Meghan. Your vocation was never a roadblock. The problem was my insecurity. I kept saying to myself, 'If this doesn't work, it's because Meghan doesn't have time to make it work,'" he told her as they looked into the Big Sioux valley. To keep himself from touching her, he clasped his hands behind his back. He didn't want to convince her through their physical need for each other that they had a future.

"You seem to be proving my point," Meghan said, sighing. His lips were thinned, strained, she noticed. He was pale. His hands were behind his back, which made the blue shirt pull tight across his chest. She loved him in blue. She just loved him.

They were standing on the place Thane most loved on the farm; the scenery below was breathtakingly beautiful. And so was the woman he'd come to love so much.

"My first marriage didn't fail because Cassandra had no time for me or for Murphy," he said. "It failed because neither of us had an emotional investment in it. Each of us was asking, What do I get out of this marriage, instead of asking, What can I give?"

He paused, reached across the cornrow and touched Meghan's arm. He would never cease loving the feel of her. When she looked at him he said, "And when you ran away from me, saying your career wouldn't allow us to have the kind of life-style I'd dreamed of, your words made me take a tough look at myself—because I had been asking you, What do I get?"

Meghan shivered at his touch. It seemed so long since she'd felt it. "Marriage is an emotional investment, not a partnership...." Her words trailed as he played his fingers over her arm, raised his hand to touch her cheek.

For the first time in three days, Thane truly smiled. "Now you've got it, sweet Meghan."

Meghan's heart bounced lightly in her chest. The longing she saw in his smile, the longing she felt... "But there is still the problem of time, Thane. I can't be a full-time wife, a full-time mother."

Thane stepped across the barrier of the cornrow that had been separating them and drew Meghan into his arms. He felt her strength, her softness, smelled the bouquet of her hair and body.

"You became Murphy's mother full-time the day you met. I saw the smiles you exchanged, the smile of love a child gives his mother, the smile of love a mother gives her child. From the beginning Murphy knew he was first in your heart. The night of the concert, he knew you were thinking about him. His old man is a slow learner, Meghan."

"You do come first in my heart, Thane. You taught me to slow down, savor the moment, but there are too few moments—"

"No more talk of time, Meghan. We're so damn good at making rules—we'll make our own rules governing time."

"What *are* the rules?" Meghan tilted her head, wanting to kiss him. Her fingers found their way to his chin, to his lips.

"No checking calendars or clocks. We simply pack a lot of quality living into the time we spend together," Thane said, kissing her fingertips. "Okay?"

"Okay," Meghan murmured. Thane's fingers were tracing patterns on her back, light pressure, heavy. She cupped his face in her hands, ran her fingers through the silk of his beard.

The sun was firing red on the horizon.

"Ah, Meghan," Thane murmured, "to me you are like the sunset on the horizon, fiery, brilliant and promising an eternity of tomorrows. Though I'm still vulnerable, because of your love, I feel secure, unconquerable."

He tugged her closer. "Sweet Meghan. Love is all that matters," he whispered throatily. "I do believe we have come to the point where we need to be engaged."

"Engaged?"

"Set the wedding date, Meghan," he said. "And for heaven's sake make it a short engagement, please."

Meghan leaned back in his arms to fully enjoy looking into his eyes. Tears slid over her cheeks. "Happy tears," she said. "I suggest September."

Thane's voice was passion-thickened. "I can't wait till September, Meghan. You have to agree that I have been *extremely* chivalrous while we were being friends and going steady."

Abruptly he turned her from his arms and strode down the hill ahead of her.

"Thane? What's wrong?" she asked as she followed him.

"Better keep your distance, Meghan—unless this isn't a platonic engagement," he said when she caught up to him. He looked at her but kept walking. "What do you say to tomorrow morning? The cows are done calving. I don't have any sows in the farrowing house."

Meghan laughed, slipped her arm around his waist. He laid his arm over her shoulder. "I take it you're done romancing me. We're being practical again?" she said. Thane nodded. She pressed her hip provocatively to his. "How about Saturday morning? Say we drive to Omaha, spend the night and come back home on Sunday."

"That's right. You'll have to be at the clinic on Monday morning," Thane said. This was happiness.

"Is a one-night honeymoon too long for you?" Meghan asked wickedly.

Her eyes were luminous, he thought, shimmering like blue honey. "No, no, I think I can handle one night alone with you," Thane said.

Meghan smiled. They hadn't kissed, but they would when the time was right. Right now it was enough to walk at his side, to savor her happiness. She took Thane's hand and drew it down over her shoulder and cradled it between her breasts. "You did say that when I'm with you the world is fiery, brilliant and promising eternity. You did say that, didn't you, Thane?"

"Did I come off sounding too romantic?"

"No, my sweet man, you didn't. I was simply memorizing the moment and your words so I can tell our grandchildren that even we old-timers had our romantic moments."

Thane laughed. "Oh, yes. I'm a true romantic. All I can think of is four days of platonic engagement and I'll be dead," Thane said, only half joking. "I need to kiss you—need . . . well, I wish I hadn't told Murphy we'd be back to tell him as soon as we set the date. He's waiting to—"

"Whoa, there. Say that again. You were so sure of me that you told Murphy we would set the date?"

Thane spun Meghan around and placed his hands on either side of her face. "I wasn't sure at all. But I did promise Murphy that if you wouldn't go along peacefully with the arrangements, I'd drag you to the altar and we'd settle our differences later."

"Well, I declare," Meghan said, feigning amazement. "You sure sound confident to me."

"Right and wrong," he said, dropping his hands to her waist, drawing her close. "I told him I didn't know how long it would take for me to convince you, so he shouldn't get the ice cream out or cut his birthday cake until—"

"You haven't let him have his cake!"

Thane kissed Meghan with all the pent-up desire and joy he was feeling. "Can't have a birthday party," he said when his lips were resting against her forehead, "until the family is gathered, now, can we?"

Before she could answer, he kissed her again, thoroughly, passionately working his lips over the accepting sweetness of her lips until he felt giddy.

Meghan came away gasping. "I don't know, Thane. Maybe a platonic engagement is a bad idea. I'm shaking in my boots right now."

"We'd better walk and talk about something else, or we're never going to get back to the house," Thane said, his voice low and throbbing.

So arm in arm they walked again, while behind them the sun, in a last-ditch attempt to stave off the night, scorched the horizon.

"Uh, talk about something else. How about—maybe I should tell you about Murphy's birthday present," Meghan said.

Thane chuckled. "I gather that's Murphy's favorite of the Donovans' litter," he said, gesturing to where Murphy was standing at the edge of the field, holding Finnigin while the puppy frolicked at his pant leg.

"It is," Meghan said. Her voice caught. "Thane, Murphy's been waiting—"

"Long enough," Thane said. To the joy he was feeling came the added joy of seeing Meghan's love for Murphy shining on her face.

Meghan raised her hand, beckoning for Murphy to join them.

With a whoop of glee, Murphy put Finnigin on the ground and came bounding to meet them. "Hey, Doc," he called, "can I call you Mom now?"

Meghan laughed while tears swelled in her eyes. "I think I'm about to cry happy tears, Thane," she whispered. "Hold me."

"Forever," Thane murmured.

Forcing her words around the tight lump of happiness in her throat, Meghan answered Murphy, "Oh, yes, Murphy, do. Do call me Mom."

* * * * *

ATTRACTIVE, SPACE SAVING BOOK RACK

Display your most prized novels on this handsome and sturdy book rack. The hand-rubbed walnut finish will blend into your library decor with quiet elegance, providing a practical organizer for your favorite hard-or soft-covered books.

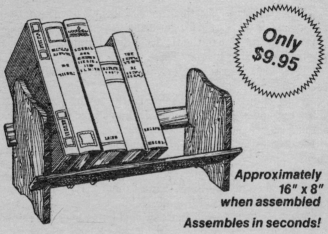

Only $9.95

Approximately 16" x 8" when assembled

Assembles in seconds!

To order, rush your name, address and zip code, along with a check or money order for $10.70* ($9.95 plus 75¢ postage and handling) payable to *Silhouette Books.*

Silhouette Books
Book Rack Offer
901 Fuhrmann Blvd.
P.O. Box 1396
Buffalo, NY 14269-1396

Offer not available in Canada.

BKR-2A

*New York and Iowa residents add appropriate sales tax.